I0671961

Mix Tape

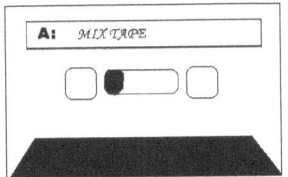

A.J Kirby

A.J Kirby

Published in 2009 by New Generation Publishing

Copyright © Text A.J. Kirby

First Edition

The author asserts the moral right under the Copyright, Designs and Patents Act 1988 to be identified as the author of this work.

All Rights reserved. No part of this publication may be reproduced, stored in a retrieval system or transmitted, in any form or by any means without the prior consent of the author, nor be otherwise circulated in any form of binding or cover other than that which it is published and without a similar condition being imposed on the subsequent purchaser.

Published by New Generation Publishing

About the Author

A.J Kirby (or Andy to his friends) is the author of three novels; the supernatural revenge novel, *Bully*, published by Wild Wolf Publishing in September 2009; the crime-thriller, *The Magpie Trap*, which was published by Youwriteon.com, and *When Elephants walk through the Gorbals*, which won third prize in the Luke Bitmead Memorial Bursary run by Legend Press in 2008. He is currently working on the dark techno-thriller *Perfect World*.

His short stories have featured in a wide number of publications, including anthologies (Legend Press's *Eight Rooms*, *Nemonymous 8: Cone Zero* & *Nemonymous 9: Cern Zoo* from Megazanthus Press, Graveside Tales' *Fried: Fast Food Slow Deaths*) print journals (Sein und Werden, Skrev Press, and Champagne Shivers) and webzines (New Voices in Horror, Pumpkin, The Second Hand, US Short Story Library, and Underground). This mix tape features some of Andy's work over the past three years.

He was runner-up in the 2008 Huddersfield Literature Festival creative writing competition, and this year was also short-listed for the Cinnamon Press short fiction prize and the Mere Literary Festival prize.

Andy's work has been described as 'vivid and intense', 'deeply disturbing', and 'intriguing'. He writes about the darker side of the street; that place that people hurry past without quite knowing why. He revels in creating unease in the reader. After entering his world, 'you may want to run up and down stairs just to calm down' as one reviewer put it.

Andy lives in Leeds, UK with his girlfriend Heidi and his incredibly noisy cat, Eric.

To find out more, or to purchase any of Andy's other published works, visit his website: www.andykirbythewriter.20m.com.

Dedication

This mix tape is dedicated to all of my friends and readers across the UK and the rest of the world. To Sam and Davoc, who provide me with creative inspiration and show me that you don't have to be a slave to full-time work for the whole of your life. To Shiv and to Tino, who listened to me discussing wanting to be a writer for so long without ever wondering why I never actually wrote. To Dave, Charlie and Mike, who accompanied me to the football and gave me plenty of ideas for daft stories. To Laura, Warren and Holly and to Alice. To Matt and Rob. And of course, to all of my family; mum and dad, Jenny, Leigh, Grandad, and last but by no means least, Heidi and Eric, who keep my feet on the ground when I'm losing it and having all kinds of ridiculous grand schemes, but who also give me the inspiration to think big and let my mind wander where it chooses...

Also, big shout-outs to each and every publisher that's seen fit to use my work; many of them are small presses and web-based organisations but handle my stories with the love and respect which they'd apply to their own writing. Small presses are the lifeblood of the publishing world, and without them, many writers would simply give up the ghost. And for these publishing concerns to dedicate so much time and energy to providing writers like me with a helping hand, whilst at the same time having a daily struggle for funding, is both awe-inspiring and selfless. I doff my cap to you all.

Mix Tape

Welcome to the first volume of the collected works of the writer A.J Kirby. Because Andy is something of a technophobe, the stories are arranged like an old-school mix-tape, or a 'Greatest Hits' catalogue. And like all good mix-tapes, they chart the mood of the party, from the excitable, laughable and crazy-ass to bitter-sweet and then maudlin, and finally chilled out...

There's something here for everyone, from straight literary fiction to horror and from fantasy to bizarre. There's love, hate, torture, murder within these pages, and much, much more.

These pieces have been published on-line, in periodicals, journals and magazines, but this is the first time they have appeared in one volume.

And like all good mix-tapes, there's a bonus, unpublished piece to watch out for...

Enjoy!

A.J Kirby

Mix Tape

Track List

Side A: Party Started: Way out West

'Day in the Life'
First published by Skrev Press in *Texts' Bones* journal: August 2007, ISBN-10: 0980133807/ ISBN-13: 978-0980133806

'No two Snowflakes are the Same'
 Featured in the 'Sein, Cos, Tan' issue of *Sein und Werden* (Summer 2008)

'The One Wish Foundation'
Originally published on-line on Huddersfield Literature Festival website (Story was runner-up in the Creative Writing Competition 2008)

'Business as Usual'
First published in *Word Weavers General Fiction Anthology 2008: Of Shadows and Substance*

'Think Tank'
Originally published on-line by *Sein und Werden*: March 2008

'Survival of the Fittest'
Third place in the *Golden Visions Magazine Freedom Writing Contest* - (story published in the July 2008 print edition - ISSN1940-817X)

Bonus Track: Unpublished Short Story

'Smokers' Corner'

Side B: From Spooked to Bitter-Sweet to Chilled

'Skeleton in the Closet'
First published in *The Thinking Man's Crumpet* magazine, February 2009

'The Sugar Footprint'
Published in on-line by New Voices in Fiction magazine and also in *Necrology* magazine (now sadly defunct)

'Me and My Shadow'
Originally published in January 2009 in *Champagne Shivers* annual magazine

'The Sticky End of the Wrong'
Published in the New Voices in Fiction magazine anthology, *Ten Nails*. September 2008

'The Allotment'
Published on-line by *The Second Hand* (US Literary journal), April 2008.

'Ten years down the drain'
Published in April 2009 by U.S website, Short Story Library.

'By Hook or By Crook'
Published in the first issue of *Underground* magazine, August 2008.

'Distance'
Published on-line in the first issue of *Pumpkin* magazine, January 2009

A Day in the Life

From: Donovan Liddell; To: H. Kirry; Subject: The Article

Harry

They sent over the article by courier today, which I read through with a great big smirk plastered all over my boat even though the greasy paper ink got all over my hands. It seems that your PR goons are doing their job for once. Sounds like I wrote the thing myself. It amused me, and that's the main point about seeing your own great ugly mug plastered all over the Sundays. I read this book when I was inside about a man that kept getting called a 'bounder' and a 'cad' by all of these birds. Well, those olde-worlde words really made me laugh. Anyway, I told the PR geeks that I wanted those words in the article, and they're in. Hell, the journo even used the term 'ne'er do well'; superb. Even Buttered Bun readers will spot the 'irony' in that, seeing as though I'm doing so well.

The 'day in the life' seems so good that I'd almost be tempted to actually do half of the stuff of my own back. Or maybe not; can't really see me 'gadding' about in an art gallery, can you? Anyway, the reason I'm writing is because I just wanted to let you know that I was a little bit disappointed by the photographs they used. Do we not have a stock library of these images? You know; me looking thoughtfully out from behind my leather mask, perched on a rock; or me staring down the barrel of another shot glass at the bar, the weight of the world on my shoulders? Come on Harry; must do better. They used to write that in my school report. Well who's laughing now?

While we're on the subject of the daily rag, I'd like to ask you where all the nice looking journalists have gone? You used to send me up such stunners that I thought they'd either faked their journo exam results, or else they'd been fast-tracked to the top; anyone would have told those pretty young things anything. I know I did. They would have got all of the best stories out far easier than the torturers. People always respond better to nice things; you know, like the carrot on a stick. Anyway, I digress; what was that thing you sent me last week? She turns up, looking like some insect. Sunglasses propped up on top of her suede like they are them massive eyes on a fly. They tell me that insects will be the only thing that survives… so maybe she'll be alright then.

If they aren't fly-eyes, they look like them bits of felt that singers put in front of microphones to stop their slobber from short-circuiting the electrics. Anyway, old microphone-eyes turned her nose up at the ciggies, so maybe she doesn't believe that it'll happen. Maybe she thinks that she's one of the chosen ones- that she's got something to live for. I wasn't about to start debating this with her though. I've got better things to do. And it's nice to actually talk to someone. Most people see me and just walk the other way, or they keep their heads down, like they are looking for their keys which they've dropped down a grid.

But old microphone-eyes, the fly, she was no good at all, mate. She didn't even go the other way - you know - when they do everything they possibly can to get on my good side. She even turned her nose up at the drink I offered her. In fact, she was no fun at all.

Must do better.
xxxx
D.

From: H. Kirry
To: Donovan Liddell
Subject: The Article

Donovan

I was sorry to read of your great distress at the fact that the journalist would not immediately suck your cock, and take on board that indeed, I must do better. But even you must admit that the same would apply to you? For example, please understand that the entire Planet group now has you on their interview black-list, as does The Globe. We haven't got that much rope left that you can hang yourself with… or anybody else for that matter.

And so to 'A Liddell Worse For Wear: A Day in The Life of Donovan Liddell.' Are you aware that in one fell swoop, you have not only managed to convince the entire nation of your sympathetic leanings towards corporal punishment, you also suggested that such punishment should indeed be meted out, "to teach them suckers a lesson", in direct quotation marks? If you are going to keep your job, then you're going to need to show some kind of human qualities. Why else do you think you were sent to the art gallery, for fine dining, and the like? If you are to be entrusted with a position of such great responsibility, then you have to show at least some measure of appreciation for humanity.

Please listen to me in this, if in nothing else. You have to start behaving properly; otherwise they are going to find somebody else to do it, somebody a little more predictable. And remember this; you'll become just like the rest of us if you lose that.

Cause for concern,

H.K

From: David Turner
To: H. Kirry
Subject: The Subject

Sir

Unpredictable would be one way of describing your Donovan; unpredictable to the world, and unpredictable to himself, even. Like a toddler who has fallen off his bike, he cannot understand his role in what has happened. He believes that things just happen to him. He does not assert any control over his surroundings, but instead just blunders through his existence as if in constant surprise.

When the subject visited me, I left him outside the consultation room, and secretly watched him through the cameras. He has a natural propensity towards violence and destruction. He takes a childish glee in defacing things- drawing on the magazine covers, daubing graffiti on the table top. The subject was observed attempting to juggle with a number of articles whilst in the room. He picked up the expensive ornaments and simply threw them up into the air, again, seeming somewhat surprised by the fact that they then crashed to the ground, to their doom.

You asked whether the subject is sane, and on some levels, he is. On a legal level, he knows right from wrong, however he chooses not to care about this. From the correspondence you have forwarded, I deduce that despite great responsibility, and fame, he has stubbornly persisted in childish behaviour. On some levels, he does this on purpose: to antagonise. But on other, more unconscious levels, he is looking for somebody to care for him.

Sir: rightly or wrongly, your Donovan has been placed in this position, and like everything else in his life, he has treated it as though it is some kind of divine accident. The world tries to show him kindness, and he only throws it back in our faces. But you can trust him. You can trust him to make the most accurate choice.

Yours,

D. Turner

From: Donovan Liddell; To: H. Kirry; Subject: Penultimate

Harry

I learned a new word earlier today: penultimate. I wish I'd heard of it earlier, I'd have used it more then. People get a bit surprised when I use long words, and stare at me as though they are waiting for my face to give them a tell that I don't know what the hell it means.

Anyway, sorry for not getting back to you after your email... I was a little bit worse for wear yesterday. I don't know what came over me. Maybe it's this whole situation that's started pecking at my suede a bit too much. You know, like I've become a leper or something. No, not a leper, more like some kind of celebrity that they're too scared to even speak to in case I use my celebrity-powers to mess with their little heads. That 'day in the life' took it out of me and all, but you can't blame me. And, by the way Harry, who's to say that I never wrong-footed that journo bird with my cutting wit and charm?   Nah, I'll be honest; I felt like a stand-up at a funeral, mate.

At any rate, so what did we do? Well, as you decided for me, it was time to show her 'the new, caring' Donovan Liddell'. I put on that fresh shirt you had sent round; the black one (so that I don't get any stains on it?) I made sure that I got changed right there in front of her in the front room. So she could see all my lovely tattoos and that scar... She was all business though, and started asking me boring stuff like: 'what's your favourite colour?' and 'who's your bird at the moment?' Right in the middle of one of her most stupid questions, I just told her it was time to go to the curry house.

Keyring and Do-Nowt came with us; I know that you told me not to bring them, but you can never be too careful these days, can you? I made them take off their leather jackets though; I can't stand it when people think that I'm getting all stuck-up having them about with me all the time. Without their leather jackets on, they look less like gorillas and more like normal human beings. People you could trust them to pick up a knife and fork without crushing them.

So we get in there, the four of us, and my tummy's rumbling like the London Underground. Keyring looks like he's going to eat the menu for Christ's sake. Do-Nowt has probably had some smoke before his shift and isn't doing anything, but his eyes look as though they might just be greedier than his belly for once in his sorry life; he wants to order everything. We all look over at this journo, who is taking an age to read the menu. Keyring asks her whether it's still a required part of the training that she can actually read. She has this thin-lipped way to her, and she just says that she doesn't even want a curry. Says she's happy with just a glass of hot water. With ice, and a lemon; have you ever heard of such nonsense before? Just hot water? What; no coffee grains in that, love? No milk? And here's me thinking that flies had good taste…

So I order the hottest curry in the house, just to annoy her; an atom bomb of a curry, and no mistake. And we also order that whole spit-roast lamb thing that they do there. The table nearly buckled under the weight of all that food; all that oily, spicy, angry food. I was so hungry that I troughed it all down, hardly even letting it hit the sides. They served us those chapattis, so I didn't even need to bother with a knife and fork; honestly, that journo didn't know where to look.

Now, some might say that it was nerves that made me so hungry, but I'd beg to differ. I just seem to have become accustomed to eating a lot. I see it as a responsibility now; almost as if I'd be letting everyone down if I didn't eat like I was on death row and it was my last meal. I farted like a trooper the rest of the day, and all. I like the smell of them; they remind me that I'm alive. When I was a kid, I used to fart under the top blanket and then waft it in front of my face like it was a big fan, and I loved that smell - like a mixture of mustard gas and Brussels sprouts; I'll miss it.

But enough of my complaining; I said I wasn't going to wallow, or waste another second of my life, and so I just grin and bear it. All the worrying? That's your job now. I've got the best job in the world; only problem is, somebody keeps making me do all this stupid PR crap. Somebody at the door mate, better go,
D.
xxxxx

From: H. Kirry; To: Donovan Liddell; Subject: Penultimate

Donovan

Many thanks for the update on your day with the journalist, and your partial explanations of why the two of you may have got off on the 'wrong foot'. I'm sure that, as you say, by burdening me, you can feel a bit better about things. I'm glad that at least I had some purpose.

I trust that the TV interview went a little better? I'm afraid I missed it because I was spending some time with my family. Actually, don't tell me… I don't need to know. As long as Mr. Kieran and Dean Howitt were out of the picture then it's OK by me - sorry, Keyring and Do-Nowt, as you so stubbornly persist in calling them.

Penultimate is a very good choice of word, Donovan. For your psychiatric report came through yesterday and you passed with flying colours. We're ready to go tomorrow, and there's nothing that can stop it now. Good PR or bad PR.

I'll see you on stage,

Yours,

Harry

From: Donovan Liddell; To: H. Kirry; Subject: Penultimate

Harry

Despite what you say, I'm not famous for nothing, and I know all about how the media can make, or break you, so you'll be pleased to know that I executed the rest of my tasks in the best possible fashion.

After the feast at the curry-house, we jumped in the limo and got driven across town to the art gallery. We got a police escort, which was nice; the only other time they've given me that was when they took me to court… Everyone wants a piece of me now though, even your poncey art-galleries. They wanted to film me opening their last exhibition, so I played up to the cameras that were there; karate-chopping the ribbon they'd put across the entrance. Everyone laughed, but I think it was that nervous laughter you keep telling me to watch out for…

I walked in the first room, and it's completely bare, just a light bulb right there in the middle of the ceiling. Probably 100 watt, when a 40 would do. No pictures, no statues, and I'm thinking that someone's got in there before us and robbed the gear. I start chuckling to myself, right there in the middle of that bare room with its white walls. And then, your journo fly buzzes up to me and she tells me that I'm only standing in the middle of the exhibit. Tells me it's supposed to be 'indicative of the emptiness of modern existence.' More like; 'lights on, nobody's home' in my opinion. Do-Nowt and Keyring were pissing themselves. Luckily the cameras weren't allowed inside to see it…

Maybe that'll be what the world will be like though. Those bare walls, the echo when you put your feet down, the whitewash. That's where the journo should have taken her photo of me; looking all moody and magnificent against all that glow. Hell, I've even grown a beard; I look like God. And where does God buy his threads? Why, Harvey Nicks, of course.

So we took a walk down there, and all the while, I thought they'll never let me in - old habits die hard. I have to admit it though, I am well media savvy, and our friend the journo cottoned on to the fact that me and the doorman go well-back. I know him from my bouncing days, but she doesn't know that, she must think I'm some kind of regular in there now… Truth is, all I ever bought from there was a packet of crisps so that I could get one of those snazzy Harvey Nicks carrier bags to put them in. When we bowled up through those fancy front doors though, expecting to hear the buzz of posh people buying, I was surprised to find that the whole place was empty. Journo tells me that they'd closed it all off, especially for our visit. So, we had a mooch around the suits section, and I made some 'ummm' and 'ahhh' noises for my own amusement, but, to be honest, the curry was starting to repeat on me.

I pegged it up to the top floor, where the pissers are, and I was desperately trying to undo my belt while I was running. I can chuckle at it now, but it was nearly coming out as I crashed into the women's bogs. I was half off the seat when my kecks finally began to come down; couldn't get them over my bloody thighs... and by that point I couldn't wait any more. I pebble-dashed the whole place, and, I admit, got some on the back of my boxers. I was stamping my feet on the ground at one point. Honestly, it was like the Battle of the Somme in there... What must the birds in the other cubicles have thought? Why not find out? I got down on my knees to take a peek under the stall - again, old habits, and all that - but it was only then I remembered that they'd closed the place to the general public.

Laughing at my own terrible memory, I decided that there'd be no harm in smashing the place up a bit then. So, I started kicking at the stalls doors, crashing them off their hinges. Then I turned the taps on, and left the sinks plugged-up. I've always wanted to do that... It's not like anyone's going to be bothered though, is it? I can do what I want, and nobody's going to say anything.... Still, it was a tad embarrassing to have stains on the back of me kecks from my 'accident'.

Where better than a clothes shop to have such an accident though? There's a ready-made supply of replacement togs right there on the shelves. I went back down to see old microphone-eyes still in the suits section. Coming down that escalator, I stared at her hard, you know the way that you do when you think that the power of your eyes alone will somehow make her turn round and look... but she never did.

I got down to where she was stood and so I told her I wanted a suit, and pronto; a black one which will make me look the part for the telly interview. She started rummaging about, as though trying to get away from me; maybe I stunk. So, I grabbed the first whistle I saw off a hanger and high-tailed it into the changing rooms. Someone had kindly left a plastic bag in there, so I rolled up my old gear in a ball and shoved them in there. Then I put on all of the new gear, and walked out a new man, ready to do business; ready to meet the world through the telly. Keyring and Do-Nowt were falling about laughing again, though, and I must admit, my new strides were pretty short. They kept saying something about my cat dying. It took me back to the playground; when someone's mam had packed them off to school in too-short kecks, they just got the piss ripped out of them for wearing them at half-mast. But Harry, there you have it: at least my kecks were in keeping with the spirit of the occasion.

All decked out in all my new clobber, what I really fancied was a game of pool and a few jars, and I must admit that we managed to even talk the sappy-faced journo into joining us for a couple of cheeky ones; although she stuck to fizzy water. According to your plans, before the telly interview we were supposed to be going to look at one of them marches they keep having these days, you know, where everyone just walks the streets not saying anything, but I just couldn't be bothered.

If the world's going to end, then what better way to see it out than completely shit-faced, trying to work out which end of the cue you're supposed to hit the ball with. No matter if you're going to be on telly that evening or not. Come on mate, I thought you'd have known that about me now.

Must do better,

D.

xxxx

From: H. Kirry; To: David Turner; Subject: The Subject

David

Donovan may know the basics of right and wrong, but increasingly I fear that I am losing the ability to tell them apart. The right that I am talking about is a moral, top-heavy rightness, which feels like justice, and which also might be right because it feels wrong.

We treat him like a lab-rat, and watch as he drowns in the power that we have, wrongfully, invested in him. We divorce him from the world, from reality, and then expect him to make this decision. What will guide him in this decision? We are supposed to let him make up his own mind, but I find that he has somehow come to see it as destiny; to make the decision is his fate.

The more I have contact from Donovan, the more nightmarish this all becomes; for I can see him now as a person, rather than as the black-hooded evil I'd wanted him to be. He's a person who doesn't question why, when he turns on the television in his compound, it always shows the same things. He never questions why the newspapers we have couriered over to him have the same news in them every day, with the only difference being the odd interview with a certain Mr. Donovan Liddell thrown in for his amusement. He never questions Keyring, sorry Kieran, or Dean (whose names he cannot pronounce) about what the hell they think about the whole thing.

He is a man who is happy to survive living on surface truths, never looking for any deeper meaning. He is a man who believes that people cannot change; they are simply born one way, and die the same way. And sometimes, I find that his innocence is inviting.

Maybe it's me that needs your services,

Yours truly,

H.

From: H. Kirry; To: Donovan Liddell; Subject: Penultimate

Donovan

I have been asked not to write to you any more; they believed that I have too much of an emotional investment in what choice you make. But what other reaction could a man have?

Before I sign off, I would just like to say that there are other decisions you can make tomorrow. There isn't just black and white; do or do not. There are other ways...

I cannot tell you any more, but I hope, in time, you come to understand why I felt that our communication was so important.

Yours truly,

H.

From: Donovan Liddell; To: H. Kirry; Subject: Penultimate

Harry

May I ask you, kind sir, what the hell is wrong with you? We used to have a laugh didn't we when you came to visit me in the nick, or when you took me to my pad to show me around. Do you know what your sulky whimpering sounds like to me? Jealousy; yes that's right, I think you are jealous of me, and of the fame I'm getting. Now, get over it, and if you want a laugh, get hold of the tape of my telly interview.

I must admit, going on that show was probably the highlight of my life. I was basically brought up by the telly - mam was usually out, dad was busy… Going down the studio was like getting to know your parents when you're older, and you realise that they're not quite the whole world. You know, on the telly, the studio appears much larger. In real life, it's like a Tardis mate; just three rows of seating arranged around the stage, and of course, the famous sofa. And the filming takes over twice as long as what you actually see on screen. You know, Barry sometimes forgets his lines and they have to start all over again. He says some pretty weird stuff sometimes as well… Anyway, I'll never really watch TV shows again without thinking about the behind the scenes action which is taking place. Everything is planned to fool you into seeing what they want you to see.

Hell, they even made my ugly mug look a bit more presentable. Before going on, I was rushed across the stage, where a load of birds were waiting. Honestly, they were like an octopus; one of them slapped on a final coat of make-up, another stuffed a microphone up my shirt (copping a feel of my scar on the way up), another asked me quick questions, and another tied my shoelace! It was like all my dreams come true… Yet more of them were firing advice on where to stand, what to say, and how to address Barry Nixon- as if he was the Queen or something. In fact, he probably is a queen, looking at the state of him.

And do you know what else? When Barry first screeched the name 'Don', and I had to come out from behind that big curtain, the stuffing was completely knocked out of me. They'd asked me to talk about those made-up anecdotes you prepared for me, but I'd lost them, so what really concerned me now was the fact that I had to try and be selective with the stories which I had picked for them in order that I didn't seem like a complete alcoholic for the audience, after all, all of the funny ones I could think of involved lorry-loads of booze.

As soon as I got on, all I could think was that this was a moment of torture which I simply had to get through. What they always say in the TV mags about your mind going blank when faced with a TV camera is true! I felt like I was pissed! One moment I was grinning like a loon as the camera panned in on my face, and the next I was sat on that big comfy sofa. It was all a blur; Barry was suddenly asking me about Norman, and I had absolutely no idea who he was talking about. He could have been speaking French for all I knew. Norman? I don't know anyone called Norman... But the Scouse charmer carried on regardless; he's seen stage fright every day of his working life.

"Come on Don," he quipped. "You must have had a few that day if you can't even remember it!" This was met by mocking laughter from the student-filled audience.

Suddenly it clicked. Barry was talking about the bar called Norman; some fur-coat-no-knickers posh-boy bar I went in once on a drinking session. So I started to tell old Barry all about it. Some suits were sat round this table which had the best view of the birds on the dance floor. My pal and me weren't having that, so we asked them, very politely to leave the table. Just our luck that they not only left the table right there and then, but they also left their full drinks. They also left something else on that table; the lottery ticket. That lottery ticket. I spied it under one of the beer-mats and stuffed it into the pocket of my jeans and then forgot about it. Instead, we got stuck into the drinks that they'd left on the table, and before I knew it, my mate and I had both fallen asleep at the table. We woke up a bit later, and all was quiet in the bar. They'd set up some giant screen in there, and were showing some lottery programme on it. It was only when I was trying to fish out the last crumpled tenner in my pocket to buy another round that I remembered about the ticket that the suits had left on the table. Honestly, it was like a magic trick the way that I pulled that winning ticket out, just as the numbers appeared on the screen; I'd won...

What a story... and I'd enjoyed telling it. Despite your fears, Barry had outed me to the world as a drunk anyway. So I started to relax. Barry asked me if I had a history of gambling, or of making tough 50-50 decisions, as if that was just another thing to add to my list of misery, along with alcoholism. I muttered something about going to the Casino and blowing the lot on black on the Roulette table. Red or black, red or black; it can only be red or black, can't it? I'll never get better odds than that, will I? In my excitement, I forgot that there's another colour on that wheel of fortune; green. Of course, that little ball spun around and around, and in that whirl of colours, I saw a flash of green and I knew from that moment on that it was magnetically attracted to the big fat zero. I hardly even had to hang about to wait for the outcome. I knew what was going to happen. But then, maybe fate has something else in store for me, eh!

And with that, Barry realised that I was some kind of stage-drunk fool who was spouting complete nonsense for the hell of it, and started asking far more simple questions, like what I thought about what I'd done, and whether I felt I deserved to be in such a position of responsibility.

"Tonight Barry (and watch it, watch how I got an irritating habit of saying Barry after virtually every word, like a footballer)… tonight Barry, I'm not worried about any of that. Tonight, Barry, all I'm worried about is having a good time, Barry, Barry."

And then I just walked off. Job done; that would be my final message to the world.

Let me know what you think, if you do get to watch it,

Cheers,

D.

Xxxx

From: H. Kirry; To: Donovan Liddell; Subject: Penultimate

Donovan

I read your rambling, incoherent message three times, through tear-streamed eyes. I was left thinking: is that all? Is that the sum total of your experience? Is that all you would do if you knew that you were going to die? Is that the sum total of all of your feelings?

You simply do not care, do you? As long as you've been on telly, had your Indian, had your pints, then everything is well with the world. But what about tomorrow? Sometimes we have to pay…

For once, I can put no PR spin on things; you truly are a lost cause. You truly are the executioner of the human race,

Yours

H.

From: Donovan Liddell; To: H. Kirry; Subject: Apocalypse

Harry

So, the way they did it, in the end, was to get me to press a button up there on the stage. Just like the National Lottery. Hardly imaginative, was it? They'd rigged up this dock off big red button in the middle of a stage they'd erected (now that's a long word I do like), and thousands of people were crowded round, watching, seeing what I'd do.

There were people in that crowd skriking, just like you, Harry, and I must admit that at one point, I thought I'd gone and all, but then I realized that I'd got a bit of dust in my eye. Do you know what some rum buggers in that crowd were up to though, eh? They were going at it. They were shagging their way into oblivion; others were drinking, or fighting. Honestly, it was enough to restore your faith in humanity.

I almost saved you all then. I almost decided that you were worth something. People actually seemed bothered about their lives, mate. They weren't just rushing to and from work like people in a cuckoo clock. Everyone's faces got a bit less grey. But if everyone thought they were going to convince me that easy, then they wouldn't have been so sexed up right then would they? If there was any doubt in their minds, well, they'd never have done it… can you imagine? You've just told your boss to fuck right off, boned his wife in front of him, and then the world doesn't end? Well, then you'd really be screwed wouldn't you?

You knew it, and they know it, and I've always known it. That when push came to shove, I'd be able to push that button. That's why I was never arsed about what I did in the rest of my life. You know; the bad things I did. I never saw them as bad, because I knew that I'd got a hell lot of pressure on me to do this one thing.

Just before I go, can you just, for one minute, stop thinking of yourself, and saving your own sorry arse? You never listened properly did you? I wanted this. Working the gallows ran in our family.

I'm off to join my dad now, and I'm sure that you'll realise that this was the only decision I could have made,
Your friend,
D.
xxx

From: H, Kirry; To: Donovan Liddell; Subject: Apocalypse

Donovan

I don't quite know what to say, and I don't even know why I'm writing this to you, despite having just watched you die… but then, I suppose, I'm only replying to your earlier email. You wrote to me believing that I was dead. And with no hint of apology, I might add.

Anyway, so by now, you'll know whether there really is an after-life, you sad fuck. You'll have gone to see Daddy so he can abuse you some more. You also might, just might have realized that you'd had the wool pulled over your eyes a little bit.

You see, public executions are back. By popular demand by people like you, I'd like to add. You, Donovan, were the executioner, as you were so delighted about, but you were also the first… victim? I hate to use that word after what you did to my children. You aren't a victim; you are a callous, cold-blooded killer, and your last act on this earth would have been to kill.

Did you really think that you had won the worldwide lottery to be the man who pushed the button to end the lives of the entire human race? Did you really fall for that? That's what I couldn't believe… Believe it or not, I actually felt sorry for you at that stage; just a little. And that's when I took that job in their PR department- to suss you out. I got the world's most eminent psychologists to come and check you out, and they all concluded the same thing; that you knew right from wrong.

And then, it was Friday 13th, and your execution. My doubts still wouldn't go away. Tell me, did you really think that you could see people 'shagging' in that big crowd, or were you just trying to convince yourself that what you were doing was OK?

And do you know what? It wasn't even that exciting. You just pushed that big red button and then you just flopped over, paralysed. The crowd loved it, of course. But they didn't love you; they loved the whole way in which you were duped a little, but mostly, they just loved seeing somebody get their comeuppance.

Yours

Harry

No Two Snowflakes are the Same

When he was born, ominous storm clouds delivered him. A crack of thunder racked through the small hospital, heralding his arrival, mewling like a kitten, whimpering as he tumbled into the world. Lightning struck the ward, short-circuiting the machinery. Everywhere was the hustle and bustle of doctors and nurses, rushing to ensure that life-support systems stayed operational. It took them a full hour to return to the maternity section, and only then did they realise where precisely the lightning had struck. The metal bars of the bed were still hot to the touch; the mother lay in a dead faint. The child, still trying to nuzzle life back into his mother's breast, turned his head to look at the new arrivals, and only then, only then did they realise where *exactly* the lightning had struck.

The boy stared back at the shocked nursing staff who gathered around the bed as though visiting a tiny antichrist. His fluffy hair was turned a shocking white, and his face was twisted into a horrific sneer; lips curled back, left eye half closed. He looked, imploringly at the nurses for help; one piercing blue eye cried 'what has happened to me? Where am I?' And then he too lost consciousness. A low rumbling moan thundered through the hospital corridors that night. The boy's father had arrived and his anguish had only one name:

"My son; a freak? It cannot be," he erupted. "What have I done to deserve such a fate?"

As he repeated his lament late into the night at his wife's bedside, he realised that perhaps he wasn't being punished for something he had done, but rather, something she had done.

The events surrounding Jackson Froid's unnatural birth quickly became the stuff of legend at the hospital. His story made all of the local papers; they called him the 'Miracle Boy', or the 'Lightning Lad'. Others, more cruelly, and certainly never in print, referred to him as Jack Frost; for his hair and his face never recovered their colour. He was forever marked too; his face frozen into a murderous grimace which made him look old beyond his years.

His mother was also, somewhat miraculously, alive, as though the shock of the lightning strike had resuscitated her heart. She was made of stubborn stuff, and knew that her survival was, in part, ensured because she had to be there for her son. She had never been, fully, of this world, but she clung onto it with the fierceness and determination which defined her people. Seeing the way in which people looked at her son; barely able to mask their disgust at his unnatural markings, she had moved him away from the bustling city, and had settled further north, amidst the frozen lakes and wrinkled mountains, somewhere where he seemed more at home.

She commandeered a log cabin on a steep mountain slope overlooking a vast panoramic valley of endless white which reflected the pallid face of her son. Even when he was angry, which he rarely was, Jackson's face would remain stiffly monochrome. You could never write a sentence about him which read: 'his face coloured in embarrassment', or 'a cauldron of red bubbled up in his cheeks.' He was a happy child though; blissfully unaware, you might say. The log cabin life sheltered him from the storms of other people, and he grew into himself. He dreamed himself a part of this vast, cold nature; he made it his playground. He fished, he climbed trees, and he read books.

More than anything, he read books. He read them like he was devouring them; with a voracious appetite which belied his tiny frame. He was constantly hungry for information; he would stalk his mother's every move on her long walk home from the nearest town, where she would raid the library on a weekly basis. He would scout from tree to tree, trying to define exactly what new treats lay in her out-sized survival rucksack. Remaining unseen, he would test his new tracking skills, sniffing out the wafting scent of her perfume amongst the tang of the shed pine cones and the freshness of the winter plants. He longed to go with her into the town, to pick his books for himself, but was expressly forbidden to set even a single footprint over the fence which formed the southernmost border of his domain. Crossing that line would bring all kinds of danger to him, his mother had told him. But her dire warnings of wandering abominable snowmen galumphing menacingly through the trees didn't scare him half as much as what she'd told him about other people. In fact, he liked to think that he had more in common with the fabled snowmen than with real men, for he read books, and even in his early years, he knew that he was not like other people. He was different; his face told its own abominable story.

Other people were like his father, that great shadowy bulk of a man that he remembered in his late-night dreams and who lurked under his bed at night, ready to catch his feet if they somehow strayed over the edge…

And then, he stopped being afraid. It must have had something to do with the unexpected present which his mother brought back from her walk that special day. He had, as was his usual routine, been scouting out her return. He had hidden himself deep within a nest of pine trees along the east bank of the snowy pathway. For some reason that morning, his mother was not using that same familiar loping gait which so quickly and smoothly got her from A to B. Instead, she kept hesitating, taking her rucksack off her back and fiddling with the straps on the top. At one point, she knelt down right in the middle of the path and seemed to be feeding something into the hungry hole at the top of the rucksack. What was she doing?

Unable to contain his curiosity any longer, Jackson began to climb one of the pine trees- he had to get a better look at this strange behaviour. In his haste, though, the boy didn't get a proper purchase on one of the overhanging branches, and with an almighty crack, it gave way beneath his weight, plunging him right down, to land, clumsily on top of his mother's crouching form and the rucksack in the middle of the path.

The rucksack barked at him in alarm, and then the white head of a husky pup poked through the straps, licking its lips. The dog leapt out of the bag and straight into Jackson's arms, and then its long tongue, its meaty breath was all over his face, licking the lightning scar. Jackson had made his first ever friend.

"Snowy!" Jackson yelled for all the hills to hear, "I'll call you Snowy!"

And then they tumbled over onto the path again, rolling in joy through the drifting snow.

His mother gave him a questioning look, and then launched a tightly packed snowball into the midst of the melee. It was the happiest moment of his life.

Memories of his mother drift back to Jackson at the strangest of times. Like when he's deep in the snow-drift of an essay, trying to right the sledge of his narrative, he'll catch a glimpse of her within the jumbled blur of type on his computer screen. He'll see her hunchback form descending their mountain, the rucksack making her appear deformed. He'll see that battered old tea-cosy hat; she never cared what she looked like, she wore anything as long as it kept her warm.

Or a scent will waft towards him, carried by the flirtatious sea air, and he'll think, 'that, that is my mother's smell'. But what he won't be able to grasp, on that dancing, ungraspable evening wind, is the whole of her. He can only see her in parts; her wise, dark eyes, her mahogany skin, her beautiful long dark hair, like a black satin headdress.

Jackson hunches on his front doorstep, hands wrapped around a steaming cup of tar-like coffee for warmth. He tries to meditate her back into existence; his mind is only half on his work, his studies. He is searching for something, in all of the numbers and figures, charts and graphs which litter the desk in his office. Somewhere in all of the secrets, and half-facts, he knows there must be an equation to magic her back into his life.

He creaks his way back to his feet, and returns to the relative warmth of his house. He has not been able to read her features in the constellations, nor has he discovered the elusive four-leafed clover. Jackson sighs, gently, and pours the coffee away, watching it cycle towards the sink, knowing why it cycles in this way, instantly expressing it in his mind as a series of numbers. He doesn't know why his mother is not with him, he doesn't know why he feels so alone in this world. And then he gathers up his duffel coat and the large, battered rucksack, and he starts towards his night-shift; his real work.

The man had a long snout and spiky white hair, one ice cold eye; the rest of his face had fallen-in, like an avalanche, becoming a permanent, bestial snarl. The local children, the wee mites, tease him because of his appearance; or perhaps it is fear. It is their fear of the draft of cold which accompanies him as he passes silently through the town; their fear of his fluttering breeze, ruffling the downy feathery hairs on their arms and legs, and mostly, mostly, on the back of their necks.

As he sneaked through the town, his snout was always red and dripping with moisture, his breath was always a cloud of dense smog. He sniffled and snuffled his way down the main street every evening, always just as dark was starting to spread like melting butter on hot toast. The rest of the world was readying itself for bed, performing the nightly rituals like a mug of cocoa, a bed-time story or locking the back door. He would stomp and stamp his booted feet to keep himself warm, but no matter how many clothes he put on; how many scarves he wrapped round his neck, how many terrible long-johns he craned himself into, he still looked cold. He gave off an air of deathly cold.

As he passed the sleepy houses, the odd curtain would twitch, and the children would look out to see the crooked man walking through the shadows, avoiding the glare of the streetlights. The curtains would swiftly be returned to position, just in case the man decided that *that night* would be the one in which he would pay them a visit. He crept stealthily past the open door of the town's one and only pub. The raucous laughter of the fishermen hurried him onwards and into the night.

And then the snow began to fall. The night air was filed with fluttering whiteness, as though a flock of silent birds were descending all around. And it was peaceful. More than any shadows, the snow afforded Jackson the cover which he so craved. He blended in; he became as one with the world. Anyone still watching him would have seen his step become lighter, his progress less halting than before.

And still he walked on; he had now left the town well behind him and was approaching the brooding forest. Anyone within earshot would have actually heard him start to talk. He talked as though he still had his trusty companion Snowy shadowing his every move.

"We'll find her tonight. I know we will," he breathed into the darkness. "If my calculations are correct then, she will be in the air tonight…"

Excited now, the man's loping gait, so much like his mother's walk, took him through the cover of trees and into the heart of the forest. Eyes were upon him, but it was only those of the small nocturnal creatures, who regarded this familiar intruder on their privacy with little interest. Once the man reached the clearing in the forest, he always took a few glances around, to see if anyone was spying from the shadows of the surrounding trees, but there never was anybody there. No *other people* anyway.

Once he was satisfied, the man would start to kick at some of the drifted snow in the centre of the clearing... and then, then if anyone was watching, they would think that he had disappeared into thin air. He vanished off the face of the earth for the hours of night-time. Then, as the bells of the distant town church's clock tower struck seven in the morning, he would appear again; like a flash- a magic trick- he suddenly was right back in the midst of the forest. And then he would stamp and stomp some feelings into his legs and start his homeward journey.

Where did he go? What did he do during the long cold hours of the December days? Only Jackson Froid knew the answer to that. And he knew the answer to a great many other things too. He was, after all, a world renowned physicist. He had become obsessed with the workings of nature; the way in which things were formed, developed, grew. What things in essence *were*. This was because he did not know what he was. He had lost his roots, and did not know where to begin to find them. No, that would not be strictly true; he did have an idea of where he could start looking; that was what he did every winter's night of his adult life.

One morning, the proof arrived in the professor's pigeon hole at the university. One minute it was not there, the next it was. The shock of seeing Jackson's familiar twisted writing was like the shock of new snow which had suddenly fallen whilst the professor's eyes were distracted elsewhere. With a heady, child-like sense of anticipation, the old man tore open the envelope and pulled out the thin manuscript, cursing the stubborn ineptitude of his twisted fingers. Reams and realms of tiny figures met his eyes; he reached over for his milk-bottle reading glasses to get a closer look, but still the proof was way beyond the professor's understanding, and so he picked up the telephone.

Answered, after only two rings...

"Jackson; your proof, it looks beautiful, but what is it?" The professor breathlessly launches into the conversation.

Jackson's high-pitched whine: "Ah, professor; I was awaiting your call. I think that I have found her... where she's always been waiting. Amongst the snow flakes. Would you like me to explain?"

Later, the professor tried to share the excitement which he felt at Jackson's discovery with one of his colleagues, a tall staid man, made cynical by a life of being not quite brilliant enough.

"His mind is otherworldly; he sees the details, the patterns which other people simply gloss over. Maybe it's got something to do with his upbringing… or rather, the fact that he had to become so self-sufficient at such an early age. He had to find his own answers. Nature taught him how and where to look…"

"Other people have traumas, professor," countered the colleague. "What makes Jackson so different? No, don't answer that; I know already. He works with nobody, nobody knows his methods… you think he's a ghost!"

Sighing, the professor continued, "I have never met him. You know as well as I do that he's some kind of hermit now. But it's as though he's been a hermit all of his life; there are no records of him anywhere. And I have tried to track him down; I have tried every school in the northern hemisphere; it's like trying to find a needle in a haystack."

The colleague gave an almost triumphant snort of a laugh, "That sounds just like one of the proofs your beloved Jackson would try to write! So what's he tried to prove this time? That pigs can fly?"

"I'll admit that his Physics are almost mystical- the questions he tries to answer are almost like a Zen koan - And the answers? Most of them he cannot ever hope to discover. But he tries! And that is the beauty of his work. Can you not see? He captures all of life on these pages…" and here, the professor fanned the pages in front of his colleague's face in rapt admiration of their content. "He makes an Art of Science."

The force of his pint glass exploding back down onto the table must have measured on the Richter Scale. He fixed his son with cold, icy eyes. His cheeks burned like the Aurora Borealis; a fantastic firework display of reds, yellows and oranges, burned upon his heavily stubbled cheeks.

"You may be my flesh and blood but you are your mother's son," he growled. Anger made him Scottish again; it returned him to his wild Highlands youth. "You are an embarrassment to me. I never wanted to see you again. You're both like pagan spirits or something; neither of you belong to this world."

He had a huge old sea chart unrolled in front of him on the table, leftover from his fishing days. He gesticulated to the edges of the map, a space which was populated by grey areas and pictures of unlikely looking monsters.

"You belong here." He pointed, once again, jabbing his finger into the liminal area into which no man should cross.

His son had a habit of talking into his chest. It is a habit which has been ingrained into him, learned through shame.

"Father; I didn't ask you to come so that we could have some kind of reunion. I wanted tell you that I have found my mother. I know where she went."

Over time, his lack of contact with other people have tautened Jackson's vocal cords; when he talks now, there is a ghostly, accent-less quality to his voice. Across the table, his father cannot stand to hear his whelp of a boy speak. He sighs; taking a long swill from the dirty brown liquid in his pint glass and promptly ignores what Jackson has just said.

"When you were born, I thought that it was cruel to keep you alive. You were so small in that incubator... You weren't even properly alive. A machine had to do your breathing for you. I went there, late at night...but she wouldn't hear of it. She told me that you deserved to live; that you would be a great person." Glacially, he levelled his stare at Jackson. "Looks like she was pretty far from the mark there, eh, lad?"

Jackson winced at the accusation. He wanted to be just like everybody else; his appearance denied him that comfort.
His father continued, more slowly now, regret tainting his gravely voice,

"Why did you come here, Jackson? Why did you follow me here, to this God-forsaken place?"

Finally looking up, "I came because it's where the snow is, father. And where the snow is, she will be..."

A memory; his mother roughly drags his arms down, down into the dark sleeves of his hated duffel coat. He hates the toothy way in which the coat buttons up; the way the sabre-tooth fangs have to be threaded through the too-small eyelets. The sleeves feel as though they are trapping him, stopping the flow of blood. Where have his arms gone? Have they disappeared? And then, then the snake-like head of his mittens pops out through the coat's frayed cuff, twisting around to face him.

"Hello Mr. Snake," his mother repeats the rehearsed, comforting words. "We're off to see the world today, so button up nice and warm." But she is saying the words without thinking now, without feeling, and he can tell.

"I don't want to go out today, Mommy. I was snug inside." He is talking into his chest, into the rough material of the coat. It feels like someone else's skin to him - maybe it will listen to him.

But she is already leading him out of the front door and into the snow. They trail small footprints away from the little house and towards the forest.

"I have to show you something." She tells him, forcefully. She has crouched down in front of him, clasping his scarf as if determination alone will make him remember, will imprint this moment on his mind.

And remarkably, it has. He can still feel her hand, bunched into a fist, resting near his heart, still gripping the scarf. He can see her hand as though it were still right there. The fist is not properly formed; the thumb is tucked underneath the four other digits. It is not a punching fist; if she were to punch someone with her hand all contorted like that, she would most likely break her thumb.

"I want to go back. I want to go... home," he says. Note his twangy American accent which drew out simple words like 'home' into an almost desperate, descending moan, like a sulky child. His accent will gradually disappear, but still, even now, when he says the word home, he lends it a great weight of yearning, the American Dream vocalised.

"We can't go back there. I'm going to take you to a better place. But I have to show you something first. Come; come to the clearing with me."

For it is a magic place, the clearing. He has always known its balding-pate wizardry. He knows nothing of the rites which go on there at night, but has felt the throbbing power of the earth in that spot. The clearing at the end of the path from their log cabin in the mountains; the clearing right by the fence which shuts him away from the rest of the world.

As they reach the middle of the clearing, the snow begins to fall once more. His mother reaches out her bare hand to catch a snow flake.

She holds her hand out to show him.

"Remember this; they say that no two snow flakes are alike. But we are. We are not like anybody else, but we are like each other. If you know that, you will never be lonely. Know that I am always there, in the falling snow. If you try and catch me, to check if this is true, I will melt though. You have to picture this moment, always, to know I am there."

He lifts his mitten towards the sky, palm outstretched, and a light spattering of snow lands on it; he strains his eyes to see but the flakes are already becoming water.

"But Mommy, why will I be lonely?" He looks up to see moisture in her eyes. Snow flakes melting perhaps, but deep down; he knows it is something more important.

"A snowflake is made up of millions of tiny particles… just like a human being is made up of many, many different things. We cannot say we are not human beings, just because some of these things are different," his mother's words are now halting. She is thinking carefully about choosing the right words - ones which he will remember for then rest of his life.

Jackson is on the phone again to the professor, his voice going up an octave in crazed excitement. "I know… I know, professor; the number of ways to make a snow flake is absolutely huge. Just like the number of ways to make a human being. But when I caught that something intangible on my microscope, I also knew that this was the one - the one to prove my theory."

"But how can you possibly know, Jackson, that you have found two snow flakes which are identical?" The professor takes a deep breath before continuing, he tries to calm the impatient palpitations of his ageing heart. "To me, it seems an impossible question… It's as impossible at one level as trying to imagine the size of a blemish on one of your fingernails in comparison to the whole universe."

Jackson pauses before answering the professor's doubts: "My research *proves* the likelihood of it happening though! It shows that there is deeper meaning in the universe!"

The professor's doubts remain: "Jackson; I'm worried about you. There's no way that you can answer the question. Try to imagine every snow flake you could see falling onto a single leaf on a tree in that forest in one day's snowfall. Now try to imagine every snow flake you could see falling onto a branch of that tree. Now try to imagine every leaf, every branch, and every tree, in all of the places it could be snowing at any one time. And then try and imagine all of the snowflakes falling at one time, and try to compare them to every snowflake that has fallen throughout history. How can you possibly hope to answer whether two snowflakes are alike? Nobody could ever conduct the research… nobody could ever find the real answer."

"But professor; you're not understanding the weight of what I'm saying." This time it is Jackson who is breathless. "In that one moment in the clearing, everything became magically clear. Perhaps that's why they call it a clearing… I felt as though suddenly every snow flake that there's ever been, or ever will be, was contained in that one which I caught. And that includes everything I've always been searching for. Of course you cannot measure a snow flake - it is a passing, transitory moment, but you can prove it was there, what it will be next, what form it will take…"

"You haven't proved it though; all of your manuscript is just numbers," the professor is becoming tired now.
"You're not grasping what I'm saying," Jackson almost shouts. "What is written into each and every number on those pages of the manuscript is the proof that it is important what we do, not what we, in essence, *are*. That was my eureka moment! We are all as inexpressible, as indefinable as the falling snow."

The professor, who has always worried that Jackson teetered on the edge of madness, replaces the phone to its cradle. He stands at the window, watching the morning's new snow begin to fall, and he wonders about this disarmingly individual genius. He wonders how he has survived for so long in this cruel world; how he has not been driven to lose his boyish awe. The glass on the professor's windows has started to freeze over; frost has crept up on it, leaving icy lipstick kisses. The professor pulls his dressing gown more tightly around himself, shakes his head as though trying to shake off all thoughts of Jackson.

And then he sees it; as his eyes settle once more on the glass, he discerns the faces of a woman and a small boy smiling back at him; cold, white, but happy faces in the condensation. Water molecules make up their detailed faces; the long, frosted snout; the woman's tea-cosy hat;

snow flakes make up their smiles, and their eyes- the most important parts. What the professor doesn't realise is that the boy's face now shows no disfigurement. What the professor does understand is that he is too late; Jackson has made his last discovery. The professor does not know whether to be incredibly sad about this, or elated, but he looks again at the faces in the frosted window, and something tells him that he should be happy for Jackson has found what he was looking for all along.

Meanwhile, in another story, the professor's colleague finds himself in the forest clearing. His head, his mind, is numb with cold, but somehow, he knows that he has finally found the place. If he can find Jackson, or find his research laboratory, then somehow some of the glory will reflect onto him. He has followed the postmark on the proof which was sent to the professor, has bribed some of the locals, and has finally managed to squeeze his size twelve hiking boots in behind the smaller, less deep prints of Jackson Froid on his way into the forest.

The professor's colleague hears the cold ring of metal as he treads through the very centre of the clearing; he has found something. He kicks away at the thin snow cover, gradually brushing away the whiteness, until he finally sees it; a door in the floor. He reaches his gloved hand for the handle, his heart almost leaping out of his mouth in excitement. And then, the door has swung open, obligingly, to let him through, and he's rapidly down the ladder and into what feels like the middle of the earth; some key, spiritual place.

His eyes gradually become accustomed to the pitch dark of the room, and he thinks that he makes out work benches, microscopes, test tubes. His heart cranks it's palpitations up one more notch. Running his hand along the smooth, igloo-like walls, he finally brushes against a light-switch, and with a deep breath, switches it on. What he sees makes him drop to his knees in a mixture of shock and awe; disappointment is in there too. He now sees that the test tubes and the microscopes he first thought he saw in the room are in fact racks of pencils and pens, paint brushes. The professor's colleague sees that the room is filled, wall to wall, floor to ceiling with pictures, drawings, paintings; all depicting one woman's face. Jackson has clearly abandoned the place in a hurry; a puddle of spilled water, freezing now, lies on the floor under the desk, his scarf is draped across it.

It is as though he has disappeared into thin air.

A.J Kirby

The One Wish Foundation

"You can't smoke in here, Gerry," snapped the waitress, without pausing from her vigorous scrubbing of the beyond-rescue Formica table at which he slumped.

The table was pock-marked with black-edged burns from a million previous cigarettes; they told the story of a million slow-burn dreams which had gradually faded away. Nevertheless, our waitress tried to wipe away those fossilised dreams. Her gigantic arse wobbled away with abandon as she brought that dirty grey cloth back and forth. Gerry cast me a baleful look, acknowledging the sheer ridiculousness of the situation. I met his eyes just once, and then lowered them again to my broadsheet, hiding behind headlines such as: 'Philanthropy or Tax Evasion? One Wish Foundation to be investigated by Government'.

We were the only customers in the café. It was getting late; many of the chairs had already been stacked on the empty tables and the ample-bosomed waitress had started to brush up under my feet a moment ago, not so subtly trying to inform me that she wanted to close up and go home. I sat in the corner and nursed my steaming coffee – so hot it never seemed to cool – and hoped that I wouldn't be noticed again for a while.

When I looked again, the waitress had taken the seat opposite Gerry and was silently watching him, daring him to light up another cigarette, which he duly did. He pulled a lamp-post long Dorchester and Gray from that familiar red packet, wedged it somewhere between the creeper-vine-like wisps of his moustache and beard and reached for a box of cooks' matches from the pile of his belongings on the plastic bench.

"Gerry – please don't do that; you can come back again in the morning. Wait for them then," said the waitress, gesturing vaguely in the direction of the café's only decoration – a faded One Wish Foundation calendar which had red-ink x's marked in every day that had passed, as though it was some kind of a countdown.

Gerry took no notice and struck the match against the side of the box with the extravagance of a conductor making his first sweeping instruction to an invisible orchestra. Light fizzed; touched the end of his cigarette, and all was well in his world again. He closed his eyes in appreciation of his first hit of nicotine. The waitress shook her head wearily – *her triple chin bouncing along for effect* - but made no real attempt to stop him from smoking. Indeed as her face turned into profile, I noted that she was wearing a look of complete and utter indifference tucked within the flabby folds. Her earlier snappy tone, her disapproval, was all for show; perhaps part of some long-practiced ritual between them.

Gerry's only response was a magnificently exaggerated suck on the dimp – *he'd already managed to suck down three quarters of the cigarette in two drags* -followed by a cloud of smoke from his dragon-mouth. The waitress coughed and spluttered a little and then produced one of those tin-foil disposable ash-trays from the pocket at the front of her apron.

"If I had one wish, it would be that you would at least use an ash-tray," she said, in a low, monotonously bored voice. "Honestly, you wouldn't do that in your own home, would you?"

Gerry snorted a half-laugh which then exploded into a fit of coughing. The three-quarters of the cigarette that he'd already chowed down - stray bits of tobacco, threads of spittle and acid-yellow smoke - erupted from some unknown point behind his beard. His whole head looked as though it was on fire. I suddenly knew where the expression 'smoked like a chimney' came from; it came from some passer-by who'd been showered by the molten lava of one of Gerry's Vesuvian coughing fits.

His whole body rattled in complaint; he became the human version of the little container in which you shake the dice in a board game. You could hear lung crash against bone, kidney against wasted muscle, false tooth against metal filling. He banged the table like a wrestler on the mat, announcing his submission: *disease, please let me out of this head-lock.*

Finally, Gerry's coughing eased into a more normal mixture of intermittent wheezes and hiccups. When even these finished, Gerry took another blast of the cigarette for good measure before thrusting it into the centre of the tin-foil ashtray with such force I thought it just might spear its way through foil, table and the flesh of the legs which were nestled underneath. Wordlessly, the waitress handed him the dirty grey cloth and he wiped his mouth a couple of times, just for appearances sake.

"I'll get you a glass of water," muttered the waitress.

Gerry grunted his disapproval of the idea.

"Don't worry; water's free in here," she said. With great difficulty she managed to extricate herself from behind the table and she waddled off behind the counter. As she passed me, I lowered my eyes still further, but still caught the tell-tale scent of grease and bleach floating luxuriantly in her wake.

With the waitress absent, Gerry seemed stuck for an audience until he remembered little old me, tucked away in the corner. He began to stare at me, occasionally mumbling something entirely incomprehensible which I suppose that I was expected to respond to. Evidently, old Gerry decided that my ignorance was not by choice, but rather because I couldn't hear him, because soon he began to shuffle across the black and white tile floor towards my table, shouting at me now.

Please let him just be going to the toilet. Please let him just pass by the table. Please don't let him try to speak to me again, said a voice in my head.

Gerry must have read the discomfort in my face but chosen to ignore it, or to exacerbate it even further. He eased himself onto the plastic bench opposite me and started to fiddle absently with the salt shaker, pouring small molehills of salt onto the table. I wished that there were other customers in here that it would be more amusing for him to pester. We were in a bus station café, for God's sake, surely there would be *somebody* that had just missed a bus and needed a warming cup of tea while they were waiting for the next one? But no, there was only one bus left. I knew that only too well.

"Buy us a brew," he said, gruffly.

I ignored him, stared even harder at the minutia of the forthcoming selling-off down of the local factory – some people stood to make millions on the deal.

"Mister: can you please buy me a cup of tea?"

I looked up from the newspaper, met his eyes. His eyelids emerged from his face like over-boiled conchiglie pasta; he looked over-tired.

"My bus is leaving soon; I've only got enough change for the fare," I said, slowly. I shook the broadsheet and held it erect in front of my face like a shield.

"Ha!" said Gerry suddenly, as though proving a point. "I've been waiting for you. You're the one, aren't you?"

I didn't answer. Gerry's crusty fingers curled round the edges of my newspaper. I felt an involuntary shudder of revulsion; when most people touch newspaper they get black ink all over their hands as though their fingerprints are being taken, in Gerry's case, his hands were *already* that black, and as greasy as tomorrow's fish and chip wrappers.

"You're one of them, aren't you?" he insisted, pulling the paper down away from my face.

"I'm not one of anyone," I said coldly, wondering where the damn waitress had gone. She needed to control her customers better. I've seen people like Gerry before, with their yawning-chasm pleading-eyes. It is no surprise that I can smell drink off him; these people have nothing to fill their holes but to pour cheap carry-outs down them.

"Ah! Don't play silly beggars. You are 'im, aren't you?"

"Leave me alone," I snarled, my well of patience now run dry.

Gerry smiled, or at least I think that he smiled. His face creased into a mess of lines and bumps, nooks and crannies; irreparable structural damage was being done to his cheek bones. I swear that I saw a lone tooth emerge from his beard.

"You thought I'd be harder to fool, eh?" he said.

I drained the last dregs of my still-scorching coffee and got up from my seat. Gerry looked at me with confusion in his eyes.

"See you later," I said, and walked to the counter.

"Come back," he begged. *We'll see about playing silly beggars now, won't we*, said that voice in my head, a sliver of cruelty in its tone now.

At the counter, I was just in time to see the waitress puff and pant her way through a door which led out to the back of the café. She was clutching a precarious tower of cleaned plates. I waited for her to deposit them on the metal surface and then join me at the till.

"Yes love?" she asked, still severely short of breath.

"I'd just like to pay for my coffee now," I said.

"*Water?*" said the woman, nonsensically.

"I had coffee…"

"No… *Gerry's* water," she said, slapping her palm against her forehead. "I've only gone and forgotten his majesty's water."

His majesty? shouted that voice in my head again. *Maybe he's one of these tramps that you always hear about that have loads of money – even a mansion – tucked away somewhere but they just like living rough. Every town's got one of them...*

"Hold on duck," said the waitress, "I'll just get his..."

"Can I pay first?" asked my real, polite-society voice. "I have a bus to catch." *I also wanted to see about watching this old tramp a bit more closely; even the most far-fetched urban myths have some sort of grounding in reality don't they? That would be my wish...*

The waitress seemed caught in two minds. Maybe she feared that if she actually did go and fill a glass with water, I'd do a runner without paying the fifty-nine pence for my own drink. Gerry seized the opportunity with both hands. Without me noticing, he'd staggered to the counter too, and was now clutching at the sleeve of my Gucci jacket as though he wouldn't let me go.

"It's 'im," he bellowed. "Don't let 'im go."

Startled, I dragged my arm away from his clutches. The waitress moved out from behind the counter and filled the space between us with her massive bulk. Gerry and I eyed each other with suspicion.

"You bloody alco," I shouted.

"Leave. Now," snarled the waitress. I waited for a moment for Gerry to leave, before realising that she actually meant me. Now I was the one confused. I pulled a pound coin from my pocket and thrust it into one of her fat hands. Angry, I stalked out of the café.

Outside, in the neon buzz of the bus station, I pressed my face against the fogged glass of the café and watched the waitress calming old Gerry down. She gave him his glass of water, and had also, for some reason, pulled the old One Wish Foundation calendar off the hook behind the counter; together, they marked a large, red 'x' in the space for today.

When he left the café, she called after him: "Don't worry Gerry; come back tomorrow! Maybe they'll show up then..."

"I can only wish," muttered Gerry as he walked away. I was following him so closely; I could hear everything that the wizened old drunk said to himself. Some people didn't deserve their One Wish.

Business as Usual

1

Ged Albiston thought himself so clever, slipping into work every Saturday morning and sending an email to his boss. He used to imagine Buck coming into work on Monday morning, seeing his email (time-stamped 'Saturday morning') and thinking; *that Albiston – he's a diligent worker.* He used to imagine Buck feeling a little twinge of guilt at the fact that one of his employees was so selflessly giving up his own time and then thinking; *that Albiston – I can count on him – I can promote him.*

Bleary, beery-eyed, Albiston logged in to the system and sent some meaningless mail about running a 'diagnostics report' and then attempted to log out of the system. Nothing happened; the computer was seemingly frozen. He tapped on the keyboard again, looked up at his dazzlingly-bright flat screen monitor and then pointlessly shuffled the mouse around the 'IT Worker's do IT better than anyone else' branded mouse-mat. An error message sprung up onto the screen; Albiston narrowed his eyes to read it, feeling his palms becoming sweaty. *What the hell had he done?* He tried the IT worker's cure-all, first line of defence: turning the power supply on and off again. But as the screen wearily cranked back into life, he was faced with the same frozen image. The same error message. 'Server Down: Your IT Department will investigate the fault.' That meant him.

He began to rock back and forth nervously; his chair squeaking in protest at his shifting bulk. He wasn't, as he'd inform you, a fat man, rather he was big-boned. If that was the case then some of his bones were bona-fide dinosaur bones. He had a strong, prominent jaw-line, which, allied to his sharp teeth, reminded some of a T-Rex's mouth. His face, pasty white from lack of sleep, was reminiscent of a police photo-fit; all of the right elements were there, but they didn't appear to have any connection with each other.

Usually, Ged Albiston's hair was pristinely combed back into a kind of slick-back gangster cut straight out of a De Niro movie; right now though, in his worry, it had started to frizz-up. Most of the tar-like wax had started to lose its hold. He took a deep breath, ran his fingers through his now dishevelled locks, and instantly regretted his pathetic ingratiating behaviour. He'd clearly have to look into the problem; if any of the Senior Managers tried to log-in remotely, they wouldn't be able to, and his email was now proof that he'd been present at Ground Zero when the problem had occurred. He couldn't very well flee the scene now.

His face started to take on that same greeny-hue of the computer monitor. He looked as though he'd just been forced to drink all of last night's pints again through a huge funnel; you know, like the funnels that they put on a dog's head to stop them biting at their own stitches. Indeed, Albiston looked as hopelessly out of his depth as one of those poor dogs. Unsteadily, he clambered to his feet, almost slipping when his ergonomically-pleasing, but not particularly stable, chair chose to spin round on its rollers. If anyone was watching him – say, the Security Guard on his CCTV monitor – they'd have seen him clinging onto the top of the chair as though it was the wall on the side of a particularly slippery ice-rink. His aching limbs shot out in every direction and the pain and frustration burned in his bloodshot eyes.

Albiston sighed and wrenched open his desk drawer, pulling out a packet of Pro-Plus, thinking; *I could probably do with something a bit more stimulating – maybe a bit more of what I had last night.* Unfortunately, however, the desk drawer was similarly as complicit in the cruel joke as the rest of the office furniture. It decided that now would be the ideal moment to throw a hissy fit. Why the hell was that term the first thing that sprung into his mind when the drawer fell off its runners and spilled most of its contents onto the floor? *Hissy fit?* It belongs in the bargain bin of ridiculously outdated terms; in fact, that's where that fucking girl from last night had probably salvaged it. "There's no need to throw a hissy fit," she'd said. And he'd laughed in her face as though she'd made the worst social faux pas possible.

Leave the damn drawer where it is, he thought, trying to pull together the various frayed ends of his frazzled mind. He had more important things to be sorting out. He silently seethed as he passed between the desks towards the server room. He tried not to look at the pointless decorations with which people had tried to make their own workspaces their own work spaces. Why the hell would you want a picture of your dog dressed as Queen Victoria? Did the woman in question really think that Buck would approach her one day and say; "Ah, Mabel (or Margaret, or Maud – whatever, it was it was one of those flowery old names which seem to give off an overwhelming aroma of lilies) I suspect that you are exactly the person we are looking for to run our new financial audit division because of your keen interest in dressing Mr. Snootles as a reigning monarch from the nineteenth century. Yes; you are without doubt the most qualified person for this difficult and demanding job. You can even bring in Mr. Snootles to uplift the team morale." Unfortunately, that would be the exact kind of *blue-sky, left-field* thinking in which Buck seemed to excel, reflected Albiston.

Maybe it would be better if he tried to cross the floor with his eyes shut. It seemed that last night's intake of beer and Class-A's had simply exacerbated his poisonous hatred for this place. He hated the open-plan, 'no-secrets' layout, the inane motivational posters, the gloomy graphs and barren bar charts. Most of all, he hated the fucking server room. It was the beating heart of the whole organisation and yet they'd chosen to house it in what was little more than a broom cupboard. Worse; because of the huge amount of electronic equipment which was in there, running 24-hours a day, the place was more like a Sauna. Well, more like the traditional idea of a Sauna, and not like the kind of Sauna Ged Albiston frequented.

His limited edition Adidas Gazelle's squeaked into the server room and the door closed behind him with a *whump* reminiscent of an air-lock closing on a space ship. As soon as he entered the server room, he knew that there was something wrong. Alert signals were flashing everywhere; the fans had gone into over-drive. It was like stepping into an action movie where an asteroid is going to smash right into the space ship, and the terribly out-dated computer tracing systems just collapse into a twitching mush of bleeps and sighs.

Yes, he thought, computer systems were fucking wimps – the slightest trace of something out of the ordinary and they turn into spineless cowards; they just shut themselves down. Hot coffee spilled on the hard-drive? *Oooooh, I can't take it!* Someone accidentally clicks on a website they aren't supposed to? *I'm going to sleep now...* Even Hal; that supposedly all-powerful beacon of Artificial Intelligence had been reduced to singing *Daisy, Daisy* at the end of *2001...*

Despite his hangover, Ged Albiston snapped into action. Where the hell was his mobile phone? He needed to call in the cavalry so that he could tell them what to do. He fumbled about in his back pocket of his Armani jeans – usually the first hiding place of the delinquent piece of shit, but the last place he thought to look – but the little fucker wasn't there. If they made mobile phones with a cord attached so you don't lose them - you know, like when kids have their mittens attached to each other by a string - then they'd sell like hot cakes. *They would sell like hot cakes*; surely that particular term has had its day. Surely it's even lower in the Bargain Bin than Milli Vanilli tapes and the expression 'hissy fit'.

Get a bloody grip, Ged. Try and grasp that there is a real live situation here. What kind of situation; a situation comedy? A football commentator's 'we're in a penalty shoot-out situation' situation? Oh God; we're in a death situation. For it was only when Ged's eyes became accustomed to the dark that he took in the reality of the situation. Slippery Pete, the slack-jawed fool, looked to have hung himself with the trailing serpentine wires which extended from the massive rack of equipment. The wires were wrapped, three... four times about his spotty little neck. Oh God... it's a suicide situation.

Slippery Pete's back was turned, but his feet were unmistakably *off the ground* and he was swinging back and forth alarmingly with the breeze from the fans. What was more worrying was the fact that his weight seemed to have pulled some of the CAT5 cables loose.

"What the fuck's happened here?" said Ged, rubbing his hand on the back of his neck in embarrassment, as though he expected Pete to turn round and grin and tell him that it was all one big joke. "Pete... Pete; you alright mate?"

Of course, there was no answer from the hanging man. Choking back the vomit, Ged Albiston touched the corpse's stiff shoulders and slowly pulled him round to face him. Pete's eyes were almost popping out of his head. He looked just like those malicious cartoons that had done the rounds; the ones which had Pete's eye on a stalk, peeking through a hole in the women's toilet wall.

2

"…is this burnin', an eternal flaaaaaaaaaaaaammmmmmmmmeeeeeeee," screeched Maud – or was it Margaret – whatever she was called, she was certainly going to be known as the woman who fell out of her dress at the wake from now on. Only, she hadn't realised it yet, and nobody in the audience had thought to tell her either. Her abhorrent tie-dye dress – no doubt home made – had fallen open at the front, and there was no knight in shining armour here to save this second Judy Finnegan.

"We have to get her off there," said Ged, although he looked pretty comfortable where he was. In fact, he'd sunk so low into his seat that he was almost horizontal.

They were seated in the booth nearest the stage in the basement bar of perhaps the dingiest hell-hole known to man. The fact that it was next door to the office however, made it difficult to avoid. A karaoke bar by day - by day? Who wants to sing karaoke in the middle of the afternoon if not the downright down-and-outs – and a 'music venue' by night, the bar had been hired out by the office as the location for the wake. No expense spared there, then.

"Fuck that; this is a fitting send off for the lad. He was always spying on the girls," replied Mark Thompson, shielding his eyes from the over-use of dry-ice. Mark was just as bulky as Ged Albiston but more the type that women would call 'cuddly'. "How can you say that this would have been what he would have wanted? You never even spoke to him; nobody spoke to the slippery little twat."

"Um, excuse me," said a voice from over Ged's shoulder. It was Buck, all greased up and ready to smarm his way around all of the disgruntled employees. "Yes, sir?" said Ged, immediately rectifying his posture.

"I was wondering if you might do me a little favour? Hmmm, yes, I'd like you to do a helicopter ride over some of the tables; do a reccy, so to speak, find out what the general vibe of the situation might be. We'll touch base later..." mumbled Buck, before sloping off into the night like the blood-sucking vampire that he was.

"Fly a helicopter!" guffawed Mark, spilling some of his pint in his eagerness to take the piss out of the man that two seconds ago he'd allowed a reverential, awed silence. "That's a new one; what the hell does that one mean?"

"He's asking me to spy for him… You know, like he does with the emails?"

"Uh?" grunted Mark, before downing the remaining half of his pint in one, marathon-runner's gulp.

"Well, you know that he monitors every email which contains his name? Asks me to monitor them, anyway…"

"Margot's just realised why she's got a draft on her titties!" interrupted Mark, slapping his thigh with delight.

Indeed, the poor woman had now fled the stage in floods of tears. Albiston reflected that maybe, just maybe, he'd have had some sympathy for her if that wasn't her customary way of leaving the office at the end of every working day. There was always something to upset the poor woman; she was like the fat girl that cries to mark the end of every party. It seemed that the sign above the coffee machine which read: 'You don't have to be mad to work here, but it helps' was more apt than even the office 'jokers' had thought. The problem was, half of the staff were not mad in the way that implied a wacky, crazy sense of humour, but were, in fact certifiably insane. Take Mark, for example; the man was seemingly a laugh-a-minute, stand-up, one-of-the-lads types, but move his stapler for a moment? You'd be looking into the dead eyes of a killer.

Buck was another one. Despite his obvious, first-impression strangeness; the way he resembled Dracula and could seemingly melt into the shadows in order to listen to your private conversations, there was something more deeply wrong about the man. There was this weird facial tic that he had developed in meetings, in which if he disagreed with what you'd proposed, he would jut out his jaw in an exaggerated, aggressive manner. This would in turn cause the veins in his neck to strain and bulge, his nostrils to flare. He looked, in those frozen moments, as though some vital cog in his head had forgotten to click into place, and some deeper, wilder instinct was about to take the place of his usual placid above-it-all-ness. Or else he looked like a small boy whose toys had been confiscated.

Albiston slowly rose from his seat, ostensibly to visit the bar, but covertly, to begin his required helicopter ride. What should he do; start whirling his arms about like he was actually trying to imitate a helicopter?

He smirked to himself at the thought. He was becoming drunk pretty quickly, and starting to find the stupidest things uproariously funny, especially the way that the barman kept eyeing up Buck.

"I'll have a brace of ales," Albiston giggled.

The barman paused from his staring and started to pour the drinks with a sigh that voiced a million complaints at a million such cocky customers.

"He likes you, you know," whispered Albiston, leaning forward over the bar. "Buck; why do you think we're having the wake in here. He can't keep away."

The barman, evidently used to Albiston's tomfoolery, chose to ignore him and stared at the foaming top of the pint. He hadn't even bothered to tilt the glass, and now most of the glass was filled with the alarmingly yellow-tinted head. As though he'd not even noticed the problem, the barman simply continued pressing on the tap, forcing more liquid into the glass until it was running over the sides. Finally, he sloshed it onto the bar in front of Albiston without so much as a smile.

"Wow, thanks," said Albiston in mock gratitude. Out of the corner of his eye, he spied three of the admin girls gossiping their way to the bar. If anyone could gauge the general feeling about Slippery Pete's death, it would be these three witches. They were the kind of girls who, at the age of seventeen, had seen and done it all. Dolled-up like that, they could all have been about thirty-five, done three years in the nick, had five kids and had them taken away by the social. God, how he detested the way everybody else fawned over them, did their jobs for them. People were scared of getting on the wrong side of this trio of ugly sisters.

Albiston watched them wheel their handbags about their heads like medieval weapons, before slamming them down onto the bar next to him.

"Gimme a *cock*tail," screeched one of the harpies, as though it was the best joke in the world.

"Aye, one of those Sloe Comfortable Screws, eh?" asked another. Albiston tried to lean against the bar as nonchalantly as he could, but looked as though he was actually either unable to stand up, or thrusting out his crotch in their general direction.

"Terrible news about Pete," he tried.

The girls continued their raucous chatter as though he wasn't even there.

"Awful about Petey," he repeated.

Still no sign that they'd even heard him, let alone that they would acknowledge his presence.

"Poor Slippery Pete, eh?" he said, gently but insistently tapping the nearest one of the Urban Coven Collective on the shoulder.

"Ah Bisto; what's your game?" she snapped, jerking her head around so that her hair flew out like thousands of tiny poisonous snakes.

"It's Albiston, not Ah Bisto... Oh, who cares; I was just saying; it's terrible what Pete did to himself..."

Suddenly the three girls were on him; they set about him with an unbeatable combination of tears, snot, hugs and muttered platitudes.

"It's a *tragedy*," cried one.

"I don't think any of us can cope," snivelled another.

"He were a lovely lad," gulped the third, through a fit of coughing; she smoked a lot that one. She looked half-cigarette.

"Come on girls, pull yourself together. Time will heal," whispered Albiston, who was uncomfortably aware that he was becoming aroused by this unlikely foursome. Hell, his hand was touching one of their breasts; well, nearly.

"We're thinking of having a collection for him; buy him a bench in the park."

"To remember him by..."

"So we can go there and think of him how he was..."

"A bench? Why, did he like sitting in parks?" asked Albiston, trying to put at least some distance between his straining cock and the distraught women's bodies.

"I don't know," muttered one of them.

"How well did you know him then?" he asked, suddenly aware that as well as being sexually excited by these girls, he was also disgusted by their manufactured emotion. They were the kind of people that had demanded a counselling service at work after Princess Diana died. As if they moved in the same circles!

Suddenly they realised that the rest of the room had descended into an uneasy silence. Lights were dimmed and one piercing spotlight illuminated the stage. Without even looking, Albiston felt all eyes upon their unlikely foursome; he flushed a deep red. Numerous cleared throats told them that they should probably stop talking. He heard somebody tapping the top of the microphone which had so recently been flung to the ground by a distraught Mavis (?); it was a rasping, desperate sound. And then, as if he was making his entrance in front of a packed Colosseum rather than a wake for a dead employee, Buck danced onto the stage.

"Ladies and Gentlemen," he began, eyes sparkling in the spotlights, his arms spread wide as though he wanted to give them all a welcoming hug, "we are here today to celebrate the life of one of our valued employees; a Mr. – ummm – Mr. Peter Slipperwick. Let me begin by saying that Pete was a team-player; the kind of person that gave one hundred and ten percent on all occasions, from – um - doing his computer work, to – um, um – his – um – general demeanour around the office."
Stifled sniggering in the audience; a smattering of applause by those who thought Buck had already run out of things to say.

"And let me ask you this: do you think – um – Pete would want you all to look so glum? No; he'd want you – all of us – to move forward – um - on a go-forward basis. B.A.U, as my father used to say; B.A.U," continued Buck, before taking a long sip of his iced water. Albiston stole a quick glance across the stage to the booth where Mark was sitting. Mark was obviously trying extremely hard to keep control of his body, which was threatening to be engulfed in one of those yawns which shake your whole surroundings like an earthquake. These were the kind of speeches they'd heard many, many times before, you know the ones; the ones which sound like he is giving a team talk before a crucial baseball match.

"I remember a young man coming into my office, oh, five years ago. His eyes were full of enthusiasm and commitment. And he asked me; what can I do for my company? He didn't ask what his company *could do for him*. And let what young Pete said be a lesson to you all," said Buck, his hands clenched into fists as though he was trying to keep a check on his overwhelming torrent of emotion. The problem was, people like Albiston had been in the company for far too long to believe that such an incident had ever happened, and even if it had, the same anecdote had been used at every leaving and retirement party, every promotion, every birthday ever since. It had become as tired in the wash as Mark's fucking ridiculous 1990's Stone Island sweater.

"Let me also remind you all that the funeral is to be held this Friday. Of course, we realise that everyone would like to go, but let me ask you this? Would Pete want the company to grind to a halt? No, he wouldn't. And therefore, in his memory, we are allowing one member of each department *only* to attend the event."
More than just a smattering of complaint from the audience; a couple of boos from the back of the room.

"But the company will be running a coach trip to the graveyard on Saturday for all employees who would like to pay their last respects," shouted Buck in desperation. A wail of feedback followed his cry. It was as though the whole P.A system felt his pain and frustration. "Now, if you'd like to make your way in an *orderly* fashion to the bar; the next round is on the company… ORDERLY! I said orderly…"

The last part of Buck's speech was drowned by the noise of the stampede. It was as though the boss had told them that if they didn't have a drink in the next five seconds, they would die of dehydration. If the floor had been a children's nursery, or a basket of mewling kittens, still none of them would have given a fuck where their spiked stilettos or their Timberland's had landed. Albiston, already at the bar, demanded a champagne cocktail and a cigar.

"I don't think the company's paying for accessories," mooned the moon-faced barman.

"It's a fucking cigar, not an accessory," snapped Albiston, before diving between the twin water buffalos of the accounts department. He had to barrel his way, head-down, through the sales team; they hunt in packs, those guys; and he took an elbow in the face from one of the admin witches. Somebody even had the nerve to squash the front of one of his Gazelles, but finally he managed to crawl through that mile of shit and reached the clean air on the other side. He felt like Andy Dufresne in *Shawshank Redemption*.

Alone in the vast savannah which was the rest of the basement bar, he struggled to understand the bubbling acidic hatred in his stomach. Why did he persevere with this charade? What would happen if he strolled into the server room one day and hung himself with the Cat5 cable? Would anyone behave differently? Would he be missed? In a way, he hoped not. To be thought of as some kind of outcast by this bunch of morons was actually a badge of honour. He knew that he wouldn't be taking advantage of the free coach to the graveyard on Saturday; knew that he wouldn't be allowed the time off for the funeral, but he didn't care. He would pay his last respects, one lone wolf to another, in his own time.

Just as he was about to walk over to the booth by the stage, Albiston caught sight of John Buck. He was shrouded in the shadows at the back of the stage, but without question it was him; he was still holding the microphone, although he'd turned it off. The man wore a deathly pallid hue, as though he'd seen a ghost, and tears were running down his face. Well, thought Albiston, that's a turn-up for the Buck.

3

Some people's idea of designer clobber is stuff which shouts its maker's name as though through a loud-hailer; you wear them and become more of a walking billboard than a person. These people would just as soon buy a cheap knock-off from Turkey if they thought they could swing it. No, not the Nike tracksuit top which, when you look closely reads Mike, but you catch my drift; the actual clothes are secondary to the name. Others prefer the simply cut shirts of a master tailor or the limited edition trainers which only those in the know will recognise. It is clothing which inspires a quick, Masonic nod on the part of the fellow wearer when you are recognised as part of a select sect. You are somebody of whom another might remark: "I like the cut of his jib."

Ged Albiston was one of the second kind of designer-clotheshorses, along with slightly older pop stars, bar owners, the more discerning footballer and the wilder kind of football hooligan. He chose his outfit to wear to the graveyard with the kind of care and precision usually demanded of a surgeon. He wore his customary Adidas – Stan Smiths this time – and tight, "well-fitted" dark Armani jeans. To top it off, he wore his new black Fjallraven jacket; he felt that it gave him an outdoorsy, but cultured kind of a look. Unfortunately however, his body shape did not take kindly to being shoe-horned into a pair of tight jeans, and he resembled a jelly which had been poured into a mould and had not set correctly. His crimson cheeks were the outward sign of the exertion which came from just getting out of the house every day wearing an outfit like that.

Nevertheless, Albiston struggled onto the bus, walking as though he had two wooden legs. Sitting down on the bus was also a pain; his jeans cut into his flabby midriff. So he chose to stand, making sure that his jacket never once brushed against any of his fellow passengers. Most of them would be going to work, but he wasn't; he'd taken the day off in honour of his visit. He still added to the atmosphere of clammy dread which resonated throughout the bus however. Like them, he hung his head in a defeated, weary way which brought to mind the images of prisoners being led to their death. One woman, standing particularly close to him, had her mouth wide open in a silent scream. A man was banging his head against the fogged-up glass of the window in one of those repetitive gestures which caged animals make. Another, younger man, was either openly crying or was suffering from a terrible allergic reaction to something – probably work.

The cattle cart jerked and screeched its own objections to going into the city; it sounded like a dinosaur trapped in a tar-pit. Even above his I Pod, Albiston could hear the complaints, the utter misery which surrounded him. He cranked up the volume and tried to close his eyes, but there was no respite. He lifted his head towards the low ceiling, hoping for some more refined air up there, but to no avail. He slumped back into his zombie-state.

With a start, he saw Pete Slipperwick in the second row of seats, staring at him. It was undeniably Slippery Pete. He had the same slack-jawed look of complete and utter incompetence about him; the kind of look which said if you hadn't told me that I had to get on this bus I would have gone on standing at the bus stop until I collapsed of exhaustion. He was in his own world, was Pete. *Was* Pete; what was he doing sitting on the 126 into town? As if in recognition of this incongruity, Pete grinned. Albiston realised that he'd never seen the lad smile before, and the misshapen, metallic mess of teeth, braces and yellowing tongue immediately told him why.

Albiston screwed up his eyes and then re-opened them; a kind of unconscious reminder of his first line of defence against a malfunctioning computer. The lad in the second row of seats was still there. He was still wearing the red raincoat and the vacant smile, only, looking more closely now, Albiston could see that it was clearly not Pete. This lad was too well-dressed; the red raincoat was North Face after all. Suddenly, the depression which had begun to tug at Albiston like a guard dog on the trousers of a fleeing paperboy, began to lose its grip. Maybe this was some kind of message from beyond the grave: *it's not your fault!*

And so it was with a new found determination that he stepped off the bus and walked up the steep slope into the graveyard at St. Luke's. The morning was brisk and he could see his breath in front of his face, but it was that kind of refreshing coldness which makes you feel alive. Maybe it was the fact that he'd not had a drink the night before, but he seemed to be clearer-headed than he'd been for a long time. He allowed the sights and smells of the real world to crowd around him; the smell of the bakery on the corner of the row of shops where he'd got off the bus, the crunch of the leaves under his feet, the shine of the conkers which had fallen onto the pavement. He even made himself leap over the low wall and took the short-cut through the overhanging trees at the side of the cemetery.

All was quiet – deathly quiet, he thought to himself – as he scratched his way up the gravel path. There wasn't even the twittering of birds in the trees; hell, he couldn't even hear the traffic from the main road. Maybe this is what the world is like if you don't have to work! It's a kind of tranquil paradise of conkers and clean air, freshly baked bread and the pleasing sound of Stan Smiths on gravel pathways. Albiston kicked away some of the loose stones with enthusiasm; he felt almost like a kid that had skived school. Almost. The fact remained that he was visiting the grave of a work colleague that had committed suicide, and he'd found the body.

Albiston was startled again by the sight of a person he would have never expected to see. Although the man was shaded by the boughs of a large oak tree which hung over some of the newest graves, Albiston's eyes were irresistibly drawn to this tall, upright figure. Maybe it was because the man was so unnaturally pale, as though he'd crawled right out from one of the most recently dug graves. And who was the person he knew that would look most at home in a cemetery? Of course, it was the unmistakable Buck.

Albiston checked his stride; he didn't want to be seen. He pressed himself close to the walls of the church; if anyone passing by *had* seen him they'd have thought him either a grave robber or somebody trying to make off with the collection plate. Buck, he saw, was unmoving. He just stood there as though in a trance, staring at what Albiston could now see was Slippery Pete's grave. The corporate logos on the numerous bouquets which were scattered around it, told him all he needed to know.

"He's allus here lad," growled a voice from behind him. For the third time in little more than half an hour, Ged Albiston nearly jumped out of his skin. *Jumped out of his skin*, you remind me, is another of those hackneyed bargain-bin phrases, but trust me when I say that at this point, it is a euphemism. OK; you want to press me on the point? You asked for it… Ged Albiston's bowels suddenly gave way in a near-explosion of shit. It was like the dam had been breached by a rampaging torrent.

"Y'OK there son?" asked the voice, insistently this time.

Albiston slowly turned around, consciously trying not to disturb the shit which he could now feel soaking into his skin. He was met by the sight of a small, weasely-looking old man whose face was as wrinkled as corduroy.

"Huh? Oh... yeah," said Albiston, sheepishly.

"You know that man?" asked the weasel, eyes narrowing, nose twitching. *God I hope he can't smell me from there...*

"He's my boss," replied Albiston, deciding honesty was the best policy. "Look, I was wondering if you might help me? I appear to have had a bit of an accident."

"Don't worry about that sunshine," winked the weasel. "It's always happening to people in 'ere. Allus getting caught short. Come along wi' me. We can find you some new kecks in the jumble no doubt."

Freshly decked out in a pair of women's jogging bottoms he'd found at the bottom of the pile which had been left for the Winter Bring and Buy Sale, Albiston finally felt his face stop throbbing with embarrassment. Maybe the fact that the trousers had an elasticated waist helped too. Weasel, who as it turned out was called Duxbury, had offered to wash his Armani jeans ready for him to collect again next time he was up at the graveyard, but Albiston had declined the offer.

"Just wash them and put them in the pile like everything else."

"They look like they're worth a few bob though, son. Sure you can part with 'em? They'll be snapped up straight away at the Sale."

"'sfine; don't think I could ever bring myself to put them on now anyway."

"What was it that scared you, if you don't mind me askin'?"

"I don't know... maybe it's Pete... Pete was the lad who died... I found his body."

"And your boss, you think he had something to do wi' it?" asked Duxbury, putting into words that dread feeling which seemed to have been creeping through the labyrinth of Albiston's bowels ever since he'd seen that unmistakeable tall figure.

"I don't know... but I'll try and find out."

4

In a way, Ged Albiston sincerely hoped that John Buck had got something to do with the death of Slippery Pete. How he'd love to bring the man down by using his own over-zealous email monitoring policy against him. How he'd love to watch the man suffer. Like most employees, he regarded his boss as somebody who would only reach for the low-hanging fruit, before passing on the more difficult parts of any project to him. Oh how Buck's name was ripe for manipulation by those office 'jokers'; they'd opted for the less obvious choice and gone for 'Pass the', which eventually became 'Pasta'. Albiston knew him by the more obviously abusive, less inventive nickname of 'Fuck'.

Fuck would've been impressed at Albiston's dedication; in work on a Saturday, yet again. He might have been less pleased if he'd known *why* his underling was there, however. He was there to start digging up some fresh graves; he was going to hack in to Slippery Pete's email account. And if anyone questioned him, he could always say that he was performing a legitimate IT function, couldn't he? Nevertheless, Albiston looked shifty. He slumped over his keyboard like a student obsessively trying to hide their answers in a maths test. He had positioned the monitor so that its contents would not be visible if anyone happened to pop in to the office on the weekend; not a likely occurrence in the first place, but better to be safe than sorry.

Hacking into the account was a breeze; he'd given employees a choice of only six passwords anyway, and Pete had picked the obvious one: 'letmein'. Once in the account, Albiston headed directly for the mails from John Buck. Had there been some kind of dispute between the two? Was there a cover-up? Was this why he'd seen Fuck collapsed in tears at the wake, and why he kept returning to the cemetery? The emails didn't contain the magic cure-all answer that he'd hoped for. Most of them were Buck's customary one-liners; the man could barely turn on a computer, let alone construct an email. They were short, snappy... yes, I'll qualify that a little better; they were rude. They comprised messages such as: 'Apple Tree project on my desk 1600 sharp,' or 'Get in here and take out my waste paper basket.' Slippery Pete seemed to have been doing almost everything for his boss, seemed to have been little more than a slave. In fact, Albiston reflected, that was pretty much Pete's role within the company. Nobody really knew what he did, they just knew that he did *everything* for 'Pasta.' Maybe he was some kind of a whiz-kid?

Finding none of the evidence he was looking for in the John Buck emails, Albiston headed for the external mails next; the ones which were from friends and family. There weren't many of them. Poor Slippery Pete was either so professional that he'd not given out his work's email address, or else he had no friends in the first place. The email folder contained none of those annoying chain-mails, no jokes, no pictures and no job applications; in fact, there was hardly anything personal at all. Albiston was ready to give up the whole investigation; even in his electronic life, Slippery Pete was impenetrable. Did the man do nothing but work?

Wait; hold on! Albiston's eyes were alerted to a new, unopened email from something called the Freedom Organisation. This was more like it; was Pete a member of some underground project? Was he some kind of green freak, or worse, a paedophile or something? Oh dear; was he *political*? Nervously, he opened the email. If he hadn't been using his fingers to manipulate the mouse and keyboard, they would have been firmly crossed.

'Pete,' it began, 'we'd like to inform you that the next meeting of the Freedom Organisation will be held on Wednesday 15th at 8pm in Meeting Room 3 at the City Library. Remember to bring along your masterpiece!'

Albiston read through the email twice. What was the Freedom Organisation? More to the point, what was Slippery Pete's masterpiece? For some reason, Albiston immediately came to the conclusion that Pete had designed some kind of bomb, as though all aspiring terrorists discuss their 'secret' plans for world domination over weak tea and stale Digestive biscuits in the ante-chambers of the local library. Maybe it was the close proximity to all of those books, but something smelled fishy about these meetings and Albiston realised with a bit of a shock that he was already making plans to attend the meeting on 15th. With a quick look at the calendar, he confirmed that the date was the coming Wednesday; he didn't need to check his own social calendar to know that he hadn't got anything planned for that night.

5

When you have somewhere to be at a particular time, but don't actually want to be there, you play semi-conscious tricks on yourself in order to delay your arrival. If you're anything like Ged Albiston, suddenly it becomes more important to tie your shoe-lace than to sprint for the bus that's just about to depart from your stop. Or the headline on the billboard which advertising the evening edition of your local newspaper becomes something that you can't possibly not know about, so you join the back of a long queue in the supermarket just to purchase your copy. Once you're at the front of the queue, of course, you realise that you're actually pretty thirsty, and so you sacrifice your opportunity to be served next by that pretty, dark-haired girl, and make your way to the back of the shop to grab a can of pop from the fridge. Then, as you amble back to the tills, you notice that the old woman who took three-quarters of an hour just to scan in your bag of frozen peas last time you were in looks unhappily neglected. You forgo being served by the robotically precise, pretty girl and instead decide to give the old woman one more chance. You wouldn't want her to be sacked now, would you?

"I'm sorry love; the till's having a hissy fit tonight," said old woman, as she turned the can inside out trying to find the barcode. Ged had already noticed that the whey-faced manager was looking on, hand-on-hips, making sure that she followed procedure.

"Just take a quid for it," said Albiston, knowing that the can of pop was worth, at best, a quarter of what he was offering. Behind him in the queue, he could hear the mutterings of discontent. He was, to judge from their exasperated responses to the hold-up, personally responsible for the ruination of their lives. If they'd not had to queue up in that Supermarket queue, they'd have suddenly decided to undertake that life-altering bungee jump, or they'd have invented something better than the wheel.

"I can't do that, ducky," said the desperate old tiller, now virtually standing on her head and shaking the can in front of the scanner as though it was a percussion instrument. "We have stock checks and audit procedure to follow." (She said the words 'stock-check' and 'audit' as though they were hallowed, unknowable terms which expressed in them the whole haloed glow of *why* the people that could perform them were, in essence, better people. To understand an audit, was to somehow *become* a leader of men.)

Give a person a pound and they can drink for a day; give a person the means to fetch the drink for themselves, and, well… the look on the old tiller's face when she finally heard the stubborn bleep of the barcode scanner was something to behold. It was as though she'd suddenly been given the means to have a better life. And so, it was with a beaming smile, that she took the evening edition of the newspaper from Ged. She swept that *Herald* past the scanner as though she were performing some victory dance. Unfortunately, there was no accompanying bleep.

"It's OK; I'll just take the pop," muttered Albiston, finally realising that although he didn't want to be early, or even on time for the Freedom Organisation meeting, he didn't want to miss the whole thing entirely. With a sigh, the old tiller popped the newspaper onto the burgeoning leaning tower of products which was rapidly accumulating at the side of her till. These were clearly the products which hadn't made it; the fallen warriors.

And so, Ged Albiston's nonchalance turned into a frantic chase to make up for lost time. He leaped onto the next bus into town and seethed his way through the uncomfortable journey, his feet tapping out the accompanying rhythm to 'I'm late; I'm late, for a very important date.' He could almost feel Slippery Pete's slippery breath on the back of his neck, whispering: 'why haven't you prioritised more effectively?' Once or twice, he turned in his seat, just to check whether he would see Pete's ghost again. Luckily, there was hardly anyone on the bus to question his strange jerky movements.

His Fjallraven jacket was stiflingly hot; sweat poured from his brow. The can of pop did little to help him. The old tiller's forlorn quest to find the barcode had resulted in shaking up the contents so much that when Albiston did finally open it, it covered him with a sticky film of plastic-smelling liquid. Maybe that was the old dog's revenge for putting her through the assault course of new tricks which she'd had to learn in order to earn a few extra pennies to compensate for her miserly pension. If so, then surely the revenge would have been better served on somebody like her manager? Surely she'd seen that punishing Albiston was as pointless as throwing a bucket of cold water over a freezing Channel-swimmer?

And wouldn't you know it? As soon as the bus deposited him safely at the stop in town, the rain started. There hadn't been any kind of indication that rain was coming; no looming clouds, no crack of thunder, no cows sitting down. Not that there were any cows in town, I'd hasten to add, but you know what I mean. Anyway, the rain proved the final push which Albiston needed in order to finally make his way into the welcoming library and into the clutches of the Freedom Organisation.

The library was housed in one of those horrendous 1950s-designed grey buildings which always look unfinished, as though the architect, de-mob happy after the war, has seen fit to do away with conventional ideas like roofs or windows. It was as though they'd thought to themselves, 'I'd like to design something different from an air-raid shelter, but unfortunately have spent the last six years of my life underground, so can't really think of anything else.' As though that wasn't off-putting enough, somebody had erected a huge luminous sign – like the desperation measures that are used to attract people into Churches these days – right outside the doors which read: 'Come inside: We'll Shape your mind!' To Albiston it seemed that they were somehow threatening to ply you with LSD, but he still pushed his way through those swinging glass doors and onto the cold stone floors inside.

"Where's Meeting Room 3?" he asked the receptionist; a mad-looking woman who was wearing a hearing aid which looked as though it was weighing her head down. Her whole body was tilted to the left, so that when Albiston looked at her, his own head had to tilt on its axis in order to avoid seasickness.

"Go down the stairs; take the corridor to the left. It's the second door on the right," she answered, accentuating every word. There was surely no way that he could avoid anything she'd said, but Albiston had been too busy looking at her monstrous breasts to take it all in.

"What was that?" he stammered, almost incomprehensibly.

"The best way is to go down the stairs. The corridor splits into two there; take the left-hand route," she repeated, even showing him which hand was his left by leaning even further over. "It's the second door on your right."

"Is that the breast way, is it?" asked Albiston, grinning.

"I heard that!" snapped the receptionist, looking even madder. Albiston's face throbbed red with embarrassment and he beat a hasty retreat. He could use such ridiculous jokes on some of the girls he met in bars; the ones who were deaf to his every comment, but could hear the jangle of money from a mile away; clearly he couldn't use them on proper people like this receptionist.

Meeting Room 3 was a sparsely decorated, sad-looking place, tattooed with tattered posters on the wall. What looked like school chairs – not exactly ergonomically-pleasing – were arranged, theatre-style in front of a small raised area which resembled the stage at the karaoke bar next door to his workplace. As he tried to steal, inconspicuously into the room, the door chose to scream its displeasure, and a number of angry eyes shot round to look at him. Why was he always the sort of person that turned up late, to a cacophony of coughs and splutters of annoyance from everybody else in the room? It wasn't like he'd come in and shouted 'I'm here!' at the top of his voice, was it?

After a brief but meaningful silence which was evidently observed by all in order to make him feel as uncomfortable as possible, the evening continued as planned. Albiston finally raised his head from where it had slumped onto his stomach in acknowledgement of his fault. He looked around the room, taking in more detail than he'd done before. As there was so little in the form of interesting features, he focussed primarily on the people. They were a pretty diverse group, too. A colony of young, angry-looking men made up the front row. They all seemed to be leaning forward in a semi-threatening manner or else they were all straining to hold back something very important which they had to say. A knot of professional people like lawyers and accountants, identified by their long coats which you can wear over suits, were stationed on the far side of the room. They were all looking from side to side in a shifty way, as though they had something to hide or as though they knew that they shouldn't really be seen in a place like that. A parliament of owlish old people were in one corner; a shoal studenty-types in the other. A murder of Goths, dressed from head-to-toe in black took up the rear, close to him. It would be a good look if the jackets were Fjallraven.

What the hell was this group? Were they some sort of secret sect which worked against the big global corporations? Maybe not, judging by the people that were in attendance. He couldn't really see that old goatish man railing against injustice, wielding the sword of violent protest. He couldn't really see that housewifey-type woman with the big, parrot ear-rings as a terrorist. Maybe he should concentrate on what they were saying...

In turn, everybody in the room was standing up and saying something. Albiston strained to hear; his red plastic seat whined as he leaned forward to catch what was being said. Evidently everyone was answering a key question – why are you here?

"I'm here because it helps me to shoo away the nightmares" said one old woman, who could have been the long-lost sister of the teller in the Supermarket. She had a haunted face and she visibly trembled as though she'd drunk too much coffee.

"I'm here because I want to find the truth," said one of the angry young men on the front row. "The Freedom Organisation is the best way of doing that."

A hum of agreement reverberated through the room; Albiston looked non-plussed.

"We can all learn from each other," agreed one of the Goths. "We can become better people and make it a better world."

Ah; this is more like it, thought Albiston.

Finally, the beige man in the beige cardigan who was sitting on the stage raised a hand to promote silence. He was clearly the Chair of the meeting, a man who actually looked like a chair, as though he was made out of some unbending wood. He radiated an authority which was so very different from that of people like Buck. His authority seemed to have been gained through respect rather than privilege.

"Thank you, every one, for your insightful comments. I always feel that it is beneficial to start every meeting with a discussion on *why* we are all here... And I don't mean why we are here on this planet... just why we've chosen to give up some of our well-earned free time to put ourselves through this nightmare."

What nightmare? What the hell is going on?

"And so, without further ado, we'll get on to the main part of the evening. The readings; and tonight, I'm very happy to announce that one of the Freedom Organisation Writing Group's longest-serving members has finally finished his opus. I'd like to invite Pete Slipperwick up here to read from 'Business as Usual.'"

Albiston looked around wildly, half expecting the ghostly figure of Slippery Pete to slip out of the shadows.

"Pete Slipperwick? Pete?" The beige Chair's pleas echoed about the library antechamber. There was a nervous rustling of feet; Ged Albiston suddenly realised that it was coming from him. Slowly, he stood up.

"I worked with Pete Slipperwick. It is my sad duty to have to tell you that Pete died two weeks ago. He appears to have committed suicide."

A reverential hush shrouded the room, but slowly, Albiston became aware of a tiny sound; the gentle sobbing of one of the student types.

"Why, why?" she begins to wail. "You worked with him, could you not see his pain?"

"What?" gasped Albiston, barely capable of collating his thoughts into anything which would go any way towards answering this girl's eternal question.

"I never knew," he said, "I never knew how bad it was."

"It was killing him! Killing his creativity; his spirit!" yelled the girl. "He used to write about it... his pain."

"I suppose he was miserable," allowed Albiston.

"He gave me a copy of his story," said the girl. "Asked me to bring it along in case he didn't dare to read it. I think that *you* should read it."

"Me?" he asked, feeling as though he was drowning.

"You're Ged Ah Bisto, I take it?"

"Umm – yeah."

The girl limped across the room, agonisingly holding out a sheaf of dog-eared paper to him: "Well, as the story's about you, I think you'd better read it out to us."

"Go on," prompted the beige Chair, like the voice of God from the stage.

The story had the look of a suicide note about it, but at the same time, couldn't have been more incriminating if it had contained the bloodied fingerprints of Pasta Buck. Ged Albiston's eyes scanned through the text before reading it aloud, trying to negotiate his way through the feelings of shock, terror and sadness which threatened to engulf him. Every word contained Slippery Pete's wispy little voice; his humanity.

"Chapter One," said Ged, softly. "Business as Usual. Today, I found Ged Albiston lying prone underneath the table of John Buck's office. I only went in there to clear out the waste-paper, and, my task complete, was about to exit the office when I saw the man's designer trainers sticking out from under the desk. At first, of course, I thought he was fixing Mr. Buck's computer terminal and that's why he was lying on the floor, but then it dawned on me; the lights were off. So what was he doing down there? Was he alive, even?

Finally, I saw his leg twitch, and I was able to breathe a sigh of relief. But I still didn't know what to do – at first, my twitching fingers reached straight for the light-switch, but then I held back. I spoke; asked him if he was okay, but I received no response. Now I know that Ged Albiston has a reputation for being a drunk, but it struck me that even he wouldn't have passed out in the boss's office. It would be more than his job was worth.

Slowly, and with great care not to startle the man, I lowered myself into a seated position on the floor by his side. Albiston barely even registered my presence. I noticed that he was humming softly to himself; the tune the White Rabbit sings in *Alice in Wonderland*; 'I'm late, I'm late, for a very important date.' It was only then that I realised that the man was clearly going through some kind of a breakdown."

Albiston felt himself swaying on the stage. He raised his hand to his brow and tried to massage the memory away. Amongst all of the beers and Class As, the Saunas and the new clothes, he'd forgotten the misery he'd faced on a daily basis… until now. How could he have forgotten such a humiliating experience? How could he have completely blocked it from his mind? Choking back the tears, he tried to continue reading, despite the writing becoming blurred.

"Albiston finally spoke to me. He told me all about Buck, and how he drained the life out of his employees until they became nothing but empty shells. To my eternal shame, I told Buck all about what Albiston said, and that's why I got the promotion instead of him." Albiston gasped; finally he knew what Pete's role within the company was – why they'd called him Slippery Pete; how had he forgotten that?

Had he been sleep-walking for the past six months? He glanced up at his audience, wondering what they were making of his performance. Eyes looked back expectantly at him; they wanted to know how this all ended.

"I thought that Albiston would leave the company," he continued, "but they gave him some time off sick, and when he came back, he was like a different person. It was like he finally allowed the infectious culture of our work place to overwhelm him; drown him. He grew a new, thicker skin to ward off the blows, to cover up that part of himself which still retained any hopes and dreams. And I had to watch this happen to him. I had to watch his spirit die.

It's a dirty little trick, isn't it, the way that we are convinced that what we really want is money, and how we can get it is by prostituting ourselves to the straight-jacket of a work suit. We sell our most creative hours for the price of a couple of pints or a new T-Shirt. How much did the devil convince you to sell your soul for? Oh, for the price of a packet of cigarettes from the vending machine. And I didn't even get the full packet. You only get sixteens from those things."

"I like that part," interjected the beige Chair with a nod. "I like the way that he expresses the sad compromise which we all have to make... Carry on – uh – Mr. Albiston."

"Chapter Two. Buck is making my life a misery. Meanwhile I watch Albiston get steadily fatter. He wallows in complacency. I cannot stand this any more; what I've done. I am going to tell Buck that it was all a lie; that Albiston should have the promotion rather than me. But then, that would simply put him in line for another nervous breakdown; I can't win. I don't know what to do. I have to find a way of letting Albiston know what I've done to him. I have to try to help him to escape."

"Read the last part!" shrieked the girl. "The final shocker; the part where Buck gets his comeuppance. It's on page 35."

Obediently, Albiston leafed through the manuscript and found page 35. Immediately, he understood.

"And the best thing about it all," he read, excitedly, "is that the stupid arse still made me collect his waste paper. That's where I found the evidence of his embezzlement of the funds from the Apple Tree project. And now he knows that I know. When I go, he won't know what I'll do with it. Hell, he'll probably try to dig up my grave to get to it."

Think Tank

Slumping merrily across tartan bean-bags is conducive to the thought process; it says as much in the Company Handbook. And so, arranged like Greek philosophers considering a particularly troublesome existential dilemma, they ponder and muse, mass debate and meditate. Oh, but it would have been fitting for the deliberations to have taken place in some clearing betwixt the stooping bows of olive trees laden with their dark fruit. Our truth-seekers could have plucked nature's bounty from the very trees, without having to stop their mental gymnastics for even a second. As it is, they have to make do with coffee and croissants; cigar-like pastries one would imagine rolled on the luscious, trembling thighs of a Marseilles virgin, if there ever can be such a thing.

And, unfortunately, their thought processes are held back by the constraints of architecture; four walls and a ceiling box them in; their flapping minds cannot soar to the full heights to which they are evidently capable. But they try; oh, how they try. Wings aflutter, they speak loftily of bottom-line figures, returns on investment and the fabled creature; the customer. Flightily, they consider how they can woo this savage beast. For let he that hath understanding calculate the number of the beast. It isn't your common or garden round figure such as ten pounds; rather, it is the magic number of nine pounds and ninety nine of your grubby little pence.

Marketing is the science of understanding human motivations and the glory of anticipation of where that fluesy, fashion, might chance to go next. It is also about having the confidence to lead; to have the utter conviction that your preachings, your soothsaying, *will* become a reality. If there were some way, perchance, of measuring the self-assurance in this room on this particular day, then that measure would record a final reading as being *way off the scale*. Oh, some talk of universities as being home to 'fine minds', but there they are not shelved properly; they are allowed to cork, to turn vinegary. Here, in this hallowed place, lie the true masters of the Wolfeian universe. Glory be, to these gods amongst men.

We enter, like shabby no-marks, and watch in awe-struck silence as they play arpeggios upon the rich threads of their majestic thoughts. We drink it in as though it is a stolen draught of heaven-juice. Six people – although I hesitate to use the pejorative *people* to describe these magicians of the soul – are in the room. They number five men and a woman. They are dressed like ancient Kings and Queens; finery of mind is embodied in finery of regalia.

Hush now, one speaks.

"If he is to be a true role-model, then we need him to better reflect the desires of kids today," says one of the men, sagely; his mane of a mullet hair-cut nods along with him, emphasising his wisdom. He is named Chris Parker and I would humbly wash his feet if he were ever to deign speak to me, a lowly peasant. "He has to have the look that they aspire to – buff like Andre, a little bit cheeky like Ant or Dec, witty like the one off *Little Britain*, but without the homo overtones, of course."

A giggle from the rest of this council of councils; they show that they are not averse to humour; they can be as other men are.

"What we need, is to get rid of the beard. At a push, we could turn it into a neat little goatee, but we can't have *that*," says a second man – Nick Hibbert - gesturing dismissively at the parchment which he has unravelled on the floor in front of him. If this scrap of papyrus is all that they have to work with, they will truly have to pull some magic out of the bag. It shows an image of a trampy-looking man wearing bloody sandals and a long beard. He has wrapped himself in some kind of sheet like they do at Halloween and, weirdly, this bright light shines out from behind his head – the illustrator should have used a flash.

"He needs to be clean-shaven. He needs to smarten up his act… He needs to look as though he cares about his appearance," says a third man. This man, if I may distract you for a moment, is John Buck; the all-powerful leader, although, as the sacred Company Handbook proclaims, everyone has a voice at one of these blue-sky thinking meetings. There is an air of the priest about the man, such is his subtle authority. He is the kind of man who looks at ease in any situation. Right now, he is lolling half-way onto the floor; most of the beans in his bean-bag have collected at the other end.

"Think of the money which will roll in if we do give him a shave… the razor companies will be all over us like a shaving rash… and they were looking for some way of launching that new one with the eight blades," says Chris Parker.

"What else?" says Buck.

"Can the tan," says Chris, star-pupil. "The guy on that paper looks kinda Middle Eastern. We can't have that in the current climate."

"Good. And?"

"Stop me if I'm speaking out of turn, but sandals? Who wears sandals these days? We're all about flip-flops and knee-length khaki shorts these days. Tight tees which show off the abs."

"Good. What about a baseball cap?"

"Too American. This guy needs a world-wide appeal."

"Okay, what about the rest of his image?" asks Buck, staring wide-eyed at the rest of the room. Is anyone else going to say anything apart from these two shining stars?

"You mean the cross?" asks Nick Hibbert. Ah, the crux of the matter.

"I'm not sure about the cross either," intones Chris Parker. "What does the word cross say to you?"

"Chart it," orders Buck, pointing at a flip-chart which is situated by the window.

Chris saunters across the room, making it clear that far from following orders, he is actually taking it upon himself to approach the flip-chart. He has a way of walking – all roll-shouldered arrogance – which reminds one of a bull mastiff. *Sure* you might get a lead on him, but he sure as hell would be doing the pulling.

"Okay," says Chris, "We think cross, we think David Beckham..."

The marker-pen squeaks across the embossed paper of the chart; Chris's writing is confidently scruffy, as though the attentive audience is so sure of him, they don't need conventions such as legibility in order to ascertain his point. "Any more?" he asks, pen hovering above the page.

"How about cross as in angry? You know; 'my parents are cross at me because I didn't do my homework,'" stutters Maud, or Maureen, or Mavis, or whatever the only woman's name was. She is there for appearance's sake only; her thoughts do not reach the levels of the others.

Buck makes a vague tutting sound in her general direction.

"The kids don't say 'cross' any more; they say something like: 'ma mutha has a beef with me cause I never did me H.W," says the tirelessly cool Dan Coppell. He is their interpreter, the man who rebuilds the Tower of Babel which allows these gods to understand the 'man on the street'. "Or they say 'ma momma cuss me cause I partied too hard.' There's a proliferation of faux-American phrases entering their vocabulary…"

"We're blue-skying a bit too far off-base," snaps Buck. "Let's get back to the P.O.E. D-Man."

"The *point of exercise* is that we think the way the kids think. We *get down* with their programme. Cross still sounds a little like cuss," says Dan; the D-Man, they call him. No, not demon, de- *man*.

"What about the *Red* Cross? Doesn't that bring to mind images of people wandering about with their arms and legs blown off?" says Chris Parker, a concerned look on his face.

"How can you wander about when you have no legs?" says Mabel or Margery or Melissa, or whatever that woman fancied calling herself. For our purposes, I shall call her Mildred from now on. I discern that this is what her name badge – still safety-pinned obdurately to her lapel after all these months – reads.

"Stop this nonsense," erupts Buck. "A cross is a cross; how do you think the Red Cross got its name?"

Chris Parker's face suddenly brightens; he has plucked an idea from the very ether. He watches the bickering of the others for a moment, full of the knowledge that he will soon become the hero of the hour. "Listen; a cross brings to mind a plus sign; positivity, addition, *more, more, more*," he says, drawing the cross on the flip-chart. "We shorten the vertical line and make it the plus sign."

"Good, good," shouts Buck clapping his hands together like a seal. More of the beans in the bag give way and he's now basically sprawling on the wooden flooring.

"Do you know what worries me? It's this whole water and wine scenario. I don't really think that's the right message for our youngsters… Remember the Vodka Ice Creams?" asks D-Man.

The audience nod sagely.

"We all remember that particular debacle. Vodka Strawberry Skulls for Halloween. A marketing master-stroke, but for those goons at the alcohol concern charities," says Buck, a tired note creeping into his voice. He sounds like a man who has discovered never-ending life but has had to shelve the plan due to pesky health and safety laws.

"Water into fruit juice, then," says Chris Parker. He's on a roll.

"Water into a delicious, nutritious shake," says Mildred. Everyone ignores her, correctly.

"Loaves and fishes ain't right either," says D-man; he's a demon for research is D-Man. "You want your Sub-Whopper Dub-Dub these days or your Allday- Everyday PigKing…"

"What about the veggies?" asks Mildred.

"Fuck the veggies!" shouts the entire room in unison. I swear that my voice complemented Buck's dusky baritone then. Wonderful!

John Buck stands up wearing the self-satisfied smile of a man who knows that they've nearly finished the job. He pours himself another coffee and paces the room.

"One more thing we need to wrestle with; the Church has asked us for new designs for the stained-glass windows. It's all a little old-hat though. I'm thinking the Nathan Coley piece in the Turner Prize. You know the one: 'There will be no miracles here.' Big flashing plastic light-bulbs. An ironic statement."

"But the whole point is that he did perform miracles. That's the basis of the belief," says Mildred, annoyingly not getting the point.

Chris Parker ignores her: "I saw this great bit of graffiti in the toilets at the football a couple of years back. 'Jesus saves, but Van Nistelrooy nets the rebound.' We need something like that."

"Why don't we just go the whole hog and dress him in a football kit then?"

Silence; reverential silence. I knew that there was something else to Mildred. She has perception, wisdom even; or perhaps she's just been lucky. Perhaps some of the wondrous brain-power of the Chris Parkers and the Nick Hibberts of this world has rubbed off on her.

"That's not a bad idea, Mildred," says Buck, rubbing his chin. "Not bad at all. They say that football is a religion… There's something to be said for this idea."

"Do you think we'll be able to get this Ruud Van Nistelrooy character?" asks Hibbert.

"We might have to aim a bit lower than him… Have you ever thought about Les Ferdinand?"

"Nope – he was rumoured to have wrecked the Blue Peter garden when he was a youngster. We need someone more clean cut…"

"What about Gary Lineker?"

"Too wrapped up in the crisp-deal."

"Oh my God," said Chris Parker, suddenly. "I think I've got it. The Hand of God himself!"

John Buck reached for the only telephone in the room.

"Ellie? Get me Diego Maradona's agent on the phone. We have our new Jesus."

Survival of the Fittest

Looking back I'm amazed that nothing like that happened sooner. The real mystery was not that it happened at all, but that it took so long for someone to crack. Too much freedom often comes at a price, and the price we all paid was heavy.

When the unstoppable force meets an immovable object, there's only one thing that will happen. That's what I told the investigating officer when he started asking me those difficult questions. That's also what I keep on telling myself when I wake up in a cold sweat in the dead of night and the devil comes a-calling, wearing the souls of each and every one of us around his neck.

The nightmare is recurring; I relive those moments when I could have chosen to go back, when I was innocent, before I saw Jim Trainor's slippery tongue nailed upon that big conference table at the Opportunity Corp headquarters...

...There are three of us in the room and we're looking at one another with these sheepish smiles which betray our lack of comprehension. None of us speak; we don't want to say or do the wrong thing. We just sit there, trying not to squeak on our high-backed leather-covered chairs, dwarfed by the daunting conference table in the centre of the room.

We've been left alone in here to watch a health and safety DVD, only the trainer has neglected to put one on. Hell, there's not even a TV screen in here, let alone a DVD player. We all know that we're being tested. They are probably watching us on covert cameras at this very moment, laughing at our shared cluelessness, our lack of assertiveness; something. Maybe, when the trainer told us about the health and safety DVD, we were supposed to come over all *Glengarry Glen Ross* and just say that we didn't care about the correct way of picking up boxes, that we were men, and we were here to survive. After all, these places are all about survival of the fittest, aren't they?

I wonder if the same thoughts are passing through the minds of the other inductees. Outwardly, they are both projecting that cock-sure stance that we all presume is expected of us, but inside? What agonies are these two going through inside? I wonder if they too feel a little cheapened by being here. Already, our qualifications have been ridiculed: "The only thing you'll need here boys, is your wit and your persistence." Already, they've told us, in muttered, brush-it-under-the-carpet tones about the fact that the pay-scale that was advertised actually being on target earnings. Without any commission, we'd be on less than the minimum wage. But that's just to make us work harder, isn't it? We should only worry about minimum wage issues if we aren't confident in our own ability to keep making sale after sale.

And so, we sit here and stew in our uncertainty, but we also weigh each other up. When afternoon comes, we'll be measured against each other. They've already told us that they will be keeping only one, at best two of us on after our trial period is over. It is like a real reality TV programme. And who am I trying to consign to the rubbish-bin of history? The slightly messy-haired boy opposite me is Danny Morris, a young university graduate who's already told us (without laughing) that he's out to make his first million before he's twenty-five. Further round the arc of the table is the other one, the smaller one, who's already confused us all with his broad Scottish accent, and amused us by asking us to call him 'Jock.' I thought the only people that went by the name of Jock were the wild drunks in the dark drinking dens around Glasgow Queen Street Station. Jock, I fear, may well be the one that is thrown back into the dole queue in a weeks' time.

Finally, the trainer marches back into the room: Jim Trainor is his name. At first, I'd thought that it was a particularly bad joke to settle our nerves. He sounds like the kind of man that your wife would have an affair with; you know, 'she's gone off with her *Gym Trainer*'. He moves to the head of the table, all rolling shoulders and bristling with arrogance. Without even deigning to cast a glance in our direction, he starts to recite more stock, company mottos again.

"Freedom," he says, elaborately rolling the 'r'. "This place is all about freedom. Here we're free to earn as much as we want, without it being capped. In what other business are you free to set your own wage? In what other business can you say "that is how much money I want to earn" and then go earn it?"

Jim Trainor pauses, as though overcome by the wonder of the word, by the glory of the opportunity that they are so kindly pushing our way. "Freedom," he repeats, fixing his eye on Jock, who looks a little scared. "You'll know all about freedom, won't you Jock, seeing as though you're from the home of Braveheart… *Freedom!*"

Trainor's impression of Mel Gibson is cringe-worthy; Jock has to pretend that he loves it though, just to keep up appearances. He must, at all costs, be seen as one of the back-slapping, pinstripe-suit wearing, hard-drinking, dirty joke loving, who gives a fuck about anyone else crowd here at the Opportunity Corp.

"Do you know who else benefits from the freedom that we facilitate?" asks Trainor.

I start to feel a twinge of sympathy for Jock as I note that he is frantically scribbling down everything that the trainer says into his reporter-style notebook. *This isn't school*, I yearn to whisper to him. He still hasn't noted the subtle shift in the room, hasn't realised that a question has been asked and that he must answer. He soon learns the hard truth though. It crashes down on him along with the trainer's thick ring-bound file of Sales Techniques which has been flung in his direction. For a moment, I fear that Jock will start crying.

"The customer," I answer, hoping to take some of the heat off my potential new colleague.

Trainor shoots me a questioning look and then continues: "That's right, Bailey; the customer. What you have to make your customer understand is that we are providing them with a wonderful opportunity. By joining the Opportunity Corp as a VIP member, they'll have access to all of the wonderful deals which we have on offer. We are the facilitators of freedom. They want that lip-smackin' insurance deal for their new Mastiff car but they've had one too many smashes in the old one? We can give them that freedom to purchase at the same rate as the old lady who never goes out apart from Church on a Sunday… Or perhaps you're calling Mr. Nicotine himself, who's smoked two hundred Dorchester and Grey every day throughout his miserable little life. He can't get healthcare unless he pays a premium, but we can give him the freedom to pay the same as anybody else. And what about Mr. John Wayne who wants a gun license but can't on account of his previous? We are the facilitators, boys."

"But isn't that… illegal?" murmurs Danny Morris, nervously.

"The license will be in our name. We would own Mr. Wayne's gun… he would have it on loan from us. What we do is we trust people to behave properly with the freedoms that we offer them. In fact, we do the opposite to the government, who don't trust us to have the freedom in the first place and therefore necessitate the illegal activity."

Trainor looks pleased with his answer. The inductees, me included, all stare back at him, slack-jawed. It wouldn't take a mind-reader to work out exactly what each of us is thinking; how can the Opportunity Corp have got away with this for so long? Do we really want a piece of this action?

"We provide the freedom for our clients to act how they want to act. We're like gods, boys, think on that," he grins. Questions and doubts continue to swirl about my mind but I can't find the right voice to translate them with. Here, such doubts would be enough to get a boot up the backside and a door closed in your face. Can I really do this? Can I really sell my soul?

One look at my battered old Sarcophagus wedged behind the bins in the car park so it can't be seen by the drivers of the sleek Mastiffs, the polished Dobermans, the brutal Rottweilers and the guffawing Hyenas tells me that I can sell my soul. And if you could see my apartment (box-room might be a better description; you virtually have to shower in the sink, sleep on the fridge and cook on the windowsill) you'd be telling me that I don't have much of a choice in the matter. I don't have the freedom to say no; beggars can't be choosers.

We can't afford to be philosophers either, although some part of me does continue to nag away, asking me whether giving everybody the freedom to do exactly what they choose is a good thing. What if poor Jock wanted the freedom to crack Danny Morris over the back of the head with the lead piping? Wouldn't Danny feel that his own freedom not to have his brains smashed-up had been somewhat affronted? Wouldn't I, as a free man myself, want to have the freedom to choose to not compete? Rubbish; it's the world we live in.

I suck on my Dorchester and Grey and curse the fact that I now have to stand outside in the freezing rain in order to satisfy my medically-diagnosed addiction. Who has the right to stop me from being comfortable while I smoke? Who has the right to take away my human rights from me? They asked us to talk a little bit about freedom in the induction training and the trainer loved it when I started to talk about smokers' rights. He told me that they really make an effort here to employ people who truly understand what it is to have a freedom taken away from them. They believe our understanding makes us better salesmen; we are more inclined to empathise with our clients.

Back in the Opportunity Corp offices, I find that I have a guilt-free bounce in my step now. My momentary doubt has passed and it's now all about the money. We go into the training room for one last pep talk, but each one of us is now itching to get out there and on the phones.

"This week, during your trial, you will be provided with fifteen leads," says the trainer. "Doesn't sound many? Well, keep calling. Keep calling until they say yes. As we've already told you, persistence is a key quality in this role. All of the people on your lead-cards have been identified as having a need for our service. They need it; who are you to stand in their way by not explaining the benefits properly or by being a poor salesman? Think of it like basketball. Does Michael Jordan stop trying to get that ball through the hoop if he gets a block?"

"No," we all chime. Jim Trainor has us just where he wants us now. He has sold us.

"And boys; if you do happen to sell every one of your fifteen, never fear. Your business does not have to come from these leads alone; beg, borrow or steal extra leads. You are also free to call your friends, your relatives. Which one of you doesn't have an Uncle Paul who likes a gamble a little too much, or a Cousin Mary that has a few too many Camparis of an evening? Who are you to deny them the Opportunity of a lifetime? Call 'em. Make 'em free. And call 'em in the knowledge that you boys can earn as much as you damn well please. How does that sound?"

Danny Morris is so excited that he drums his fist on the conference table; Jock McTavish looks as though he is going to explode with joy. Even I, cynical old Darren Bailey, feel like I've had a shot of adrenaline straight to the heart.

The sales floor of the Opportunity Corp offices is a windowless, open-plan savannah of space which is populated by the individual booths which are like Sheep-pens. The first thing that hits you is the noise; hundreds of men virtually chewing their headsets off, they are so pumped-up. You can't make out individual voices yet, just this clamour of staccato baritone building up into crashing waves of excitement. McTavish, Morris and I look on, overwhelmed, hardly able to think.

Close by, a man with huge islands of sweat under his armpits suddenly leaps to his feet, smashing his headset down onto his desk. "Sale!" he yells. "Fuckin' sale!"

With that, he starts this mad dash down one of the aisles, making for the back of the office. He is making this demented whooping noise as he runs. When he reaches the back of the office, he starts to clang this old bell. The act has an air of humiliation about it, but I can't quite place who is being mocked. Is it the salesman himself, or is it the customer, for being tricked into parting with their money?

"That's how we get their blood pumping," whispers the trainer. "Everyone now knows that Michaels has made a sale; that he's got one-up on them. They work all the harder now. And by the way, Michaels is the owner of that fine-looking hatch-back Riviera Sport out in the car park."

Everything here is measured by ownership, by being seen to own the best car, for example. Looking at heart-attack-waiting-to-happen Michaels and his sweat-problem, I'm not even sure how long he'll have to enjoy ownership of such a woman-magnet car.

Eventually, Trainor leads us to our own booths. They are separated from the rest of the cattle-market so as to be closer to the watchful gaze of Trainor in his office. He literally plugs us all into the company phone system and then provides us with our script, stack of leads and two large marbles. McTavish looks questioningly at Trainor, but I already know the answer before the great man can speak.

"They are in case you don't manage to grow your own balls on the job," he winks, and then leaves us to our fate.

What follows is almost too painful for me to relay to you, but suffice to say, we all have a baptism of fire. After a few moments of nervous twiddling with the wire of my headphones, I finally bite the bullet and make my first call, only to be met by the voice of an irate company director on the other end of the line. A few, brief seconds later, I hear his phone being slammed down. Welcome to the life of a telesales operative.

Amazingly, I soon learn how to overcome the initial objections from my potential customers. Soon, I'm managing to get half-way down my spiel before they hang up. A couple of times, I even get to the point where I ask for their Credit Card details. But slowly and surely, my stack of fifteen leads dwindle away, and soon I'm calling relatives and friends, hoping they'll help me out in my time of need.

Things are worse, if anything, for poor Jock McTavish. He manages to plough through his own leads in record time and I've already heard him pleading with his father or some other disapproving family member on countless occasions. With each failure, his appearance becomes more and more dishevelled. He is sweating now; worse than Michaels ever was. He looks close to tears.

Oh, the signs are there all right. It's just that I am so concerned with my own hide that I can't even see the pain that poor Jock is in. I can't see the wood for the trees. At the end of the day, we are all called back into the training room by Jim Trainor for a de-briefing session. He makes us all sign Non-Disclosure forms and then grills us all on our lack of sales. He has us just where he wants us; desperate; ready to do anything just to feel the light of his smile shine upon us once more.

"When I started work here, do you know how long it took me to make my first sale?" asks Trainor. "Five seconds; I signed myself up. I got myself in the habit of filling out the Credit Card details. Tell me; have any of you morons has the ingenuity to do that?"

And so we all do. We all sign our lives away just so we can look good in Trainor's eyes. The only problem is this; when Jock McTavish sells himself down the river, he is selling to one of those very same people that have been blacklisted from every other credit company and gun-license group. When McTavish signs that form, the first thing he does is get the Opportunity Corp licensed for a gun, which he duly picks up.

Of course, when the investigating officers come in, after the fact, they can only assume that Trainor had shot himself, seeing as though his joke-name is written across every license document going. What the investigating officers still don't know is the fact that Trainor might have been able to shoot himself, but he wouldn't have been capable of removing his own tongue and then nailing it to the conference table. I haven't seen McTavish again after that day, but Trainor's removed tongue tells me everything that I need to know about what happened.

Smokers' Corner

Brett's cigarette describes a perfect arc as he nonchalantly flicks it towards the flower-bed. Every move the man makes has an air of precision. Even if he'd not have been aiming for the sad little rose-garden, the sheer deliberateness of his movements convinced you that he had been. It was as though even the cigarette dimp was in league with him in his ongoing mission to prove to the world that he was a god amongst men. *His* cigarette ends weren't the subject of the downright petty memos which had circulated the office in recent months...

We used to be able to smoke inside, you know. We were allowed our simple human right, and productivity wasn't affected. Now, they watch us like hawks as we slope out of the office, down the stairs, through the car-park, across the road and into the Company gardens. We try to cram ourselves into the bus-shelter type construction. The wind is always blowing straight at us, as though the builders were specifically instructed to punish us smokers; make our lives as miserable as possible until we gave up.

In the office, they set their stop-watches. They go out and inspect the state of the gardens; they send us memos which complain that we are leaving too many dimps on the floor of the shelter. If we'd been allowed to continue to smoke in our office, then we'd have used ash-trays, like any other civilised human being, but treat us like animals? That's how we'll behave.

Except these new rules don't seem to apply to Brett; I've smelled his office. I know that he still has a crafty cigarette in there. No, strike that, he probably openly smokes in there, and the boss probably sees him, gives a little appreciative nod and says: *that's Brett; rules don't apply to Brett*. Not for Brett the indignity of standing on a toilet seat, trying to strain your neck up to the air-vent in the roof to blow out your smoke. Not for Brett the prescription of nicotine gum to wean you off the habit. Not for Brett these constant bloody memos, human resources meetings and instructions to see a counsellor.

So why's he out here then? Why, when he can perfectly well smoke in the comfort of his own ergonomically-pleasing director's chair?

He's like that sometimes, I suppose; likes to show that he's one of the people. Despite being of the same rank as me, he somehow makes you feel as though he's doing you a favour by deigning to talk to you, breathe the same air as you. And I fall for it hook, line and sinker every time. I try to impress him; I know that I do. I try to convince him that I've as much right to the pay-check as he does. I can feel myself doing it now; I've straightened my back, puffed out my chest and have adopted that disinterested look which suits me so well when I try it in the mirror.

But then I catch a glimpse of myself in the tinted, reinforced glass of the shelter, and know that my attempts to frame myself as 'the man' have been doomed from the start. The wind, you see, has practically dismantled my hair-style. What was this morning a slick, metropolitan look has become a kind of hurricane-battered shanty town hanging on for dear life on the edges of my head. For some reason, Brett's hair resembles a well-manicured golf course; even the sand bunkers of his bald patches seem to lend him a statesmanlike air.

Bloody hell, the man is consummate; *all* framework. His grey, professional appearance, his smooth, deliberate actions and even his dialogue have long since had everybody fooled. Look at him now, as he taps the bottom of his soft-pack and a cigarette obediently pops up, ready for him to take. The cigarette is practically begging to be burned at the altar for this slippery charlatan. If I'd have tried the same smooth bar-room trick, the whole batch of cigarettes would leap from the pack like lemmings, screaming *god, no, don't let me near his mouth!*

His second cigarette lit, Brett finally looks at me and sighs. I have the sudden feeling that he actually feels uncomfortable, as though he's struggling to say something. I look back at him, expectantly, but he fails to speak. Has the man been struck dumb? Is he finally falling apart, like I've seen so many do, working here? His eyes evade my cold, questioning stare and instead adopt a glazed-over expression, as though he is contemplating some majestic arresting view and not the wind-battered Company rose garden.

"How are things with you, Holton?" he finally asks, still staring straight ahead.

"Oh, you know," I say, not wanting to commit to either side of the life's shit/ life's bearable debate until I've seen the hand that Brett wants to play.

"What do you think of the new computer systems?" he probes.

I take a long drag of my cigarette before answering. I've smoked it right down to the end and the heat nips at my fingers; I need one of those cigarette-holders.

"Don't get me started," I lie, patently pleading for the final push which will induce me to commence my diatribe against this framework of new fangled terms and conditions, rules and regulations, databases and systems which have conspired to make my life at the Company a misery.

"It's not how it used to be, is it?" prompts Brett, looking shifty.

"Honestly, I thought computers were supposed to make life easier," I begin, grinding the finished cigarette under my foot as though underlining my frustration. "And yet, here we are, working late after every job, entering pointless data on *four* different databases. The same information! Four times! It's beyond me why they can't just put it all into one content management system, instead of one for the accounts department, one for HR, one for sales and one for the bloody marketing department."

"It's different software; we can't possibly integrate them all," mutters Brett-as-King-Canute, trying to hold back the tide of my irritation.

"I know why they've brought in this new system too," I say, wagging my finger. "It's because it can interact with the software which the Americans are using. Of course, they wouldn't change all of *their* data to correspond with ours, would they? No; despite the fact that we're doing them a favour by letting them have access to our information, they have to push it one step further and get us to change *everything* we do, just so we fit in with them."

"Hmmm," says Brett, non-committally. He is fiddling nervously with his lapel and still won't look at me.

"You said things aren't what they used to be, and you're right. Things used to be so simple when all we had to do was fill in our job-dockets by hand at the end of every job. Hell, you could even do it in your car before you drove home. Then, all you'd have to do is stick it in the post and forget all about it."

"And your next job is on your doormat when you wake up," he says, and I'm sure that I can detect a superior sneer in his voice.

"Don't get me wrong, I can see the benefits of a paperless office; automatic invoicing, job-generation… the information framework at your fingertips."

"But you preferred the old ways."

"Yes I preferred the old ways. I feel as though I'm on constant trial now. There's always system audits, new legislation… it's as though they are trying to catch us out," I say, surprised at my own honesty.

"Why would they be trying to catch us out?"

"Well… it's easy to make mistakes on these new systems… hit the wrong key and you could change an entire job…allocate the wrong person…"

"Horton; are you telling me that you don't like this new system; that you haven't been completing all the forms properly? That you've made mistakes in entering the data?"

Why is Brett repeating everything I say? Suddenly I realise, too late, that the boss has put Brett up to this questioning session. He's probably listening to my complaints via a transmitter which is hidden in Brett's lapel or something. Brett is repeating what I say in order to double-check that all of the incriminating evidence has been captured by the boss. You can't trust anyone around here.

I leave Brett at the bus-shelter and trudge back over the road and into the car park. I crouch behind one of the big four-wheel-drives and look back over at him. He appears, at first, to be hugging his trench-coat around him as protection against the buffeting wind and relentless rain, but I'm sure that his mouth is moving. Maybe he's talking to the boss through his transmitter. I reach for my trouser pocket and pull out my receiver, hoping to intercept the signal, but I'm greeted by a series of low whoops and moans. Brett must be using a new encryption code. I long to dash the little crappy object onto the diesel-slicked concrete floor, but think better of it; my last pay-check barely covered the state-of-the-art satellite navigation system which, in a fit of pique, I threw out of the car window.

I should just let it pass. That's what my counsellor always tells me; let things pass. Everyone spies on everyone here; we have files and files of information on each other which we drip-feed to the boss, hoping that next time, *we* won't be the ones passed over for promotion.

And I hate it. I absolutely loathe this atmosphere of distrust which it creates, but then, like everybody else, I store up the email proof of another's wrongdoing. I am prepared to *do somebody in* to further my own career.

Wearily, I creak upright and head out of the car park and back into the office. I'm greeted by one of the new breed of employees around here, one of the marketers.

"Holton; done your SOP report yet? We need the figures for the POA projection," she says with an inane grin on her rosy-cheeked face. She's pretty, but her constant use of acronyms has rendered her untouchable in my eyes.

"I still have two databases to go; RUG- BI and SC- ILL," I say. She's got me at it now; the goddam acronyms. We never had any of them in the old days. Back then, System Convergence – International Liaison Level was the far simpler 'talking to the Yanks' and Remote Undertaker Generator – British Intelligence was the issue of your next job – so you didn't even have to set foot in the office.

"They're the ones we need. The Americans need the KILL ratios."
Here, I'm afraid to say, the marketing woman wasn't talking in code; kill ratios were exactly what they sounded like.

"Um… I can get them done quicker if I have some help?" I plead.

"I'm not here to type," she says bitterly with that same moony smile slapped all over her face.

Well, what the bloody hell is she here for then? She's one of this new breed of support staff which the Company is seemingly hell-bent on hiring; head-strong types. There was a time when operatives like me coming into the office would have been treated with due deference, as though we were celebrities or something. There was a certain respect then, for people who went out there, put their necks on the line and did the messy jobs which kept the Company running – kept them all in jobs. Now though, some of these girls behave as though their own jobs, working with computers and figures, data and projections, are the thing that keeps the company going. Hell, they look down on people like me as though I am simply a manual labourer or something.

I need another cigarette. I've only been back in the office a matter of seconds, and already I want to be back out there with the wind and rain biting at my face. I resist the admittedly tempting urge and reach for a nicotine gum instead. I'm going to have a Desperate Dan jaw-line one of these days, the amount of these little tablets I munch on. My counsellor joked that I looked like a cow chewing on the cud. My counsellor! How about that for encouragement to carry on smoking if even your own shrink says you look stupid when you attempt the alternative to a cigarette?

But chew on the cud I do. I take all of my anger out on that piece of stinking gum, relishing the sourness of the taste, the gluey clag which builds up in the corners of my mouth. If they won't let me smoke in here, then they'll have to face the clearly revolting vision of my face twisting and contorting itself around the gum. I only wish that I could type as quickly as I can chew.

When I type, it takes ninety-seven percent of my concentration to make sure that one hundred percent of my chubby pointing finger is not pressing down on the wrong key, or, say twenty-five percent of its bulk has not strayed onto an 's' for example when I'm trying to press an 'a' or a 'd'. My keyboard is sticky, too, with the remnants of the thirty three percent of all suppers I've had to take while catching up on my paperwork in my own time, and because of the fact that I hit the keys with a force that they've not been manufactured to endure. A million one-inch punches have scrubbed the white ink from the 'n' key altogether now, and the exclamation mark has been downgraded to a full-stop. With this in mind, I can concentrate with about, say, ten percent of my full mental powers when I'm entering all of the information about my last kill onto the SC- ILL databases. I'm at it now; staring blankly at the keys, wondering from what forest of letters the 'j' will finally emerge. Maybe that's why I must have hit the 'h' key. Maybe that's why I suddenly saw my own file appear on screen in front of me.

Frantically, I smash down the escape button, but all I manage to do is turn on the Caps Lock. Escape… escape… escape. I keep pressing the button and nothing happens. Why can you never escape with escape? What is it there for otherwise; to offer you the hope of a way out and then to deny it? Is it there to mock you? I could get in a lot of trouble for accessing my own records here. Right now, alarm signals are probably going off in the manager's office. Brett is probably laughing to himself about how he's made me so paranoid that I've done the unthinkable and looked at my own file just to check whether anyone's after me…

A wave of tiredness hits me. Suddenly I don't care any more. I don't care what will happen to me if I look at this file. It's *me* for God's sake. Am I not even allowed to look at myself? And so look at myself is what I do. And look. And look. At first I am shocked by the picture which they've stored on file. It's one of me stooping on the front step, reaching gingerly for the morning newspaper. You can see a roll of my fat peeking out from a gap in the towelling dressing-gown which I'm wearing. My hair is not so much a shanty town but a stone-age village which has, in the past, been engulfed by a rampaging muddy river. My head is the excavation site. It's a shocking photograph. Why have they chosen this particular one? We're always told that the pictures they use are the ones which are most representative of the allocated person. We usually get them when they are at their weakest, you see, when the framework shows through.

I delve deeper into the records. What else do they have on me? Of course, they have all the usual; the stuff which we have on everybody. There's bank account details, health records, insurance claims, marital status, address, where I holiday, where I buy my cigarettes, how much I drink; the standard stuff which makes up a man's life. I'm surprised to see that they found out about my foot fetish porn habit, however. I thought that I'd covered that up pretty well… And that police caution I received when I was in my teens. I thought the slate had been wiped clean, but yet here it is, 'Drunk and Disorderly' for all to see. There's also a record of every conversation I have had with my counsellor; it's all there – my jealousy of Brett, my distrust of everyone, the fact that I can't type. Is this why the marketing girls view me with such contempt? Have they all seen my file and laughed at my secret hopes and desires?

I always knew that I wouldn't reach a ripe old age, but that's part of the reason I wanted to work here so much. It promised adventure; live fast, die hard. It promised so much… Now all I want to know is how they'll do it. They've long ago taken my spirit; what retirement present have I got in store for me? Somehow, I always knew that it would be nicotine that got me. I just never realised that it wouldn't be cigarettes. It's the gum, you see, the gum. They got me to go see that counsellor and he prescribed the gum to help wean me off the habit. Little did I know that they were laced with poison. Well, I always knew that I wouldn't be presented with a carriage clock here. The gum'll have to do.

Skeleton in the Closet

Though my view is distorted by the horizontal lines which criss-cross in front of my eyes, I can see almost three-quarters of the bedroom. Though I have tried and tried not to look, I cannot resist, nor avoid taking a peek at what's going on in the room. My eyes attempt to bore through the distance between us and burrow into his psyche; I try to make him nervous.

From my vantage point I can see his hairy wrist handcuffed to the frame of the bed. The metal must chafe against his skin there. He could never wear the watch I bought him; claimed that the fools' gold irritated his eczema. He doesn't look as though he's complaining now though. A thick, vacant smile is slapped across his face and he appears to be breathing heavily. There is an arrogance in the way that his bare feet tap against the wood at the foot of the bed; expectant.

Anticipation is one of the qualities I've lost; I'll never feel the hairs on my arm stand to attention as I see his sausage fingers about to brush against mine. It's not like I've had a limb amputated, but rather that it was never there in the first place. My sense of touch is gone and now unimaginable. But I can feel cold. Or rather, I can taste its sourness within the very marrow of my bones. In here it's dark and lonely; I'd pay to listen to his stories now.

It feels as though I'm so far away, but actually, I'm still in the room, only somehow, I'm invisible, forgotten about. My ghostly breath chills the air and fills it with my brooding presence. I watch him betray me over and over again. I watch him sully the sheets of our bed. I watch him at his weakest moments when he cannot find the words to express his thoughts. I watch him as he descends into that moonlit depravity which he thinks nobody else can see or know.

Through the slats which cross in front of my wide-open eyes, I see him as nobody else can; he is a little boy, unsure of how to carry himself. I watch him struggle to dress, I watch him staring out of the window. I watch him as he really is. He prefers the company of the well-thumbed pages and the splattered criticism of his jism tells him which images to leaf through to. He whispers their names; 'Lola', 'Daisy'; they are always strangely quaint names which would remind me more of my grandmother. But his mind has been warped by pornography, so the only memories they spark for him are of surgically enhanced body parts, writhing flesh and matted tissue paper. I'm within those pages; those pages which contain the smell of sex and death. I've become a part of his fantasy world too; it's just that he just cannot see me.

He keeps tissues by his bed. They are concealed in a box which looks as though it has writing paper in it; image his prime concern as per usual. He's obsessed with the image he portrays. Right now, he is radiating a superior sense of pride, and he knows it; his bulbous red bell-end rings with it. Meanwhile, I am an empty vessel, free from bodily desires, or so I'd like to think. My back leans against the cold brickwork and I watch. I always watch. I feel that I am closer to him by watching.

I am meek and not given to rash actions. And here I am, watching. I've let myself go. I don't wash my hair any more; clumps of it are starting to fall out. My sallow skin is starting to loosen over my bony body. I don't have breasts any more. I feel numb; unable to move, or to react. And his betrayals continue. I've seen that bitch in the room with him, her face pushed roughly against the pillow as he shouts out to her in his made-up alien language like a child with attention deficit disorder. He rips at her knickers, with otherworldly spittle foaming at his excitable mouth. He stops, as inspiration assaults him, and rushes to his desk to scribble some more of his ridiculous new story, his penis still erect, rests self-importantly on the edge of the paper- watching through one eye.

He's standing in front of the desk now. From my vantage point, he is side-on. His paunch is developing, and the coating of muscle which he was once so proud of, is turning to flab. He no longer has to rely on his body in order to woo women into here though, nor does he ever have to explain his morbid fetishes any more. He is famous and he can do as he pleases. He thinks he is writing his autobiography… He'll fictionalise his life – make it erotic, as though he were whispering across the valley between the pillows in bed; as though he wanted to make the reader jealous of his sexual liberty.

I know the truth; that it is disgustingly normal. Right now in his story, he makes that woman savagely drag her fingernails across his chest. His brutal grin continues. Meanwhile, my fingernails are dropping out. It's very painful. It feels as though it's all part of his torture.

The monotony of the pornography which I'm forced to endure has now numbed me to the pain of seeing him with another woman. I still admire the breathless canine way he vibrates his way in there, and then rolls away sated. It is a task to be performed for him, nothing else. Even he is bored. He unconsciously strokes his testicles as he uses his other hand to lever a cigarette from ash-tray to mouth. Then, his bowels loosened by the laxative qualities of nicotine he creeps to the bathroom.

Now, alone in the room, the naked woman starts to stroll around. She is what some people might describe as painfully thin; her rib-cage forms a larger mound on her chest than her breasts, her knees knock together when she walks, her hip-bones form a devastatingly unsubtle two-fingered salute. But I know the real bone-crushing ache of the skeletal frame; to me, this woman is fat.

She steals furtive glances at the writing he's been doing. She actually laughs at it, and I feel somehow protective of him - she shouldn't be doing that, right here, in his inner-sanctum where he's most vulnerable. Once, I laughed at his work… Then she moves closer to the closet, scrunching up her nose as though trying to sniff something out. She draws closer and closer. And then he's back in the room, and he is roughly dragging her away from the closet.

"Why does it smell so strange in that corner of the room?" I see her mouth moving, and I lip-read the words even from my distance.

"No reason. Get back into bed," he drawls.

"But it does smell awful; it smells like something crawled in there and died," she persists, not noticing the menacing leer which has crept into his eyes.

"Why doesn't it open?" She has moved back to the door and is twisting at the handle. "I'll clean it out for you if you need. You probably haven't got the time, spending all of your time writing or researching as you do…"

I will that she cannot open the door; I don't want to be discovered in here. At least here, I am kept alive, if only to be tortured by what I can see. I don't want to be found, but want to rot away in peace. This brash woman cannot find me out. I don't want to be nothing; here I am a bad smell, a memory; a skeleton in the closet.

Because she is now standing closer to the closet, it is easier to see the woman's whole profile through the slats. She looks a lot like I used to look, before I laughed at his work. I wish that I could close my eyes to the scene which plays itself out once again before my eyes, but I have no eyelids any more. Once again, I see him laugh right back at her, calling her fat. He's right, you know, she is fat, but she doesn't need to know this; the knowledge kills her. It makes her sick; she runs to the bathroom to throw up again.

Once again, I see my life end. I haunt one particular moment in time, a recurrent nightmare. If this is the only way I can live, then so be it. This will be his punishment; he knows now exactly what he is.

The Sugar Footprint

It was Frank Sheldon that set in motion the whole chain of events. Maybe it wouldn't have got so bad if Frank had let that foreign object keep on floating in the copper tank. Maybe if one of the other, less keen-eyed guys had been on the night shift they wouldn't have even seen it at all, let alone raised the alarm. But the thing must have wanted to be found; why else would it have chosen to bob up to the surface on Frank's watch? For Frank was renowned as the most dedicated of all of the Funnels Fine Sweets staff, and he wouldn't ever let it be said that something had been allowed to spoil the batch while he was on duty; he had the children of the world to answer to.

Most people couldn't stand to work a whole night in the boiling room, but Frank wasn't most people. It was said that Frank had worked at the factory since before most of the others were born. It was said that Frank would have lived in the factory if he'd been given the chance; he was that dedicated. It was said that sugar flowed through his veins. And maybe that's why the item chose to surface when Frank was standing over the Pear Drops vat. It must have sensed the complete indifference on the faces of the other workers as they masturbated into the mixtures, flicked bogies into the fizzy cola bottles and crapped in the caramel. The object picked its moment wisely when it surfaced near Frank.

It was hot in the factory that night, but then it was hot in there every night. Sweat poured down Frank's child-like face and then crystallised there into a sticky red smudges on his nose and cheeks. Spots adorned his chin like squashed jelly sweets. Although his glasses were fogged-up, it made little difference to his sight because the whole place was coated in a thick fog of sugary steam. His white coat was drenched in it too, and it reflected multi-coloured prisms of light back into the vats.

Frank was carefully noting the fluctuations on the temperature gauge when the thing caught his eye. Through the hot mist and the coloured liquid, he saw something sparkle fresh and white; an obvious anomaly. He tugged the large wooden paddle from the wall and plunged it into the cauldron, stirring through the thick layer of scum on the top to try and reach the object which was even now sinking further away from him. Summoning all of his strength he could he dragged the paddle underneath the object and directed it back towards the surface. With a dexterity that belied his bumbling form, he quickly reached for, and grasped, the fishing net from where it was clipped to the side of the vat. Like a man trying to use a giant tea-strainer and a butter knife with which to eat soup, Frank attempted to extricate the object from the vat. Leaning over, almost plunging into the broiling broth, Frank fought the erupting volcano and finally won. The object was out of his batch.

Frank followed procedures to the letter; rather than simply disposing of the foreign object, or even identifying it himself, he called Mr. Duckworth on the intercom.

"Mr. Duckworth?" stammered Frank, still out of breath from his exertions.

Silence; Mr. Duckworth must have been engaged in some vital paperwork, or else he'd be performing a spot-check inspection. Frank waited a couple of minutes and then pushed the green button once more. Finally, a tired, frustrated voice answered the call.

"What is it Sheldon?"

"It's me; Frank," said Frank, pointlessly.

"I know it's you; there's only you on tonight in the boiling room. What is it?"

"Mr. Duckworth; I have found something in the batch. I don't know what it is."

"You're always finding stuff in the batches. Can't you just let it alone? What is it this time; another bit of plastic?"

"We can't have anything spoiling the batch; that's why Funnels are known throughout the world for having the purest sweets…"

"Don't quote the damn health and safety manual at me… look; tell me what the object is and I'll decide whether we have to throw the whole damn batch into the river."

"It's a bit weird, sir; it looks a bit like a bone."

"Keep your hands off it for now, Sheldon, and I'll be down pronto," said Duckworth, before there was a loud crackle of static. He'd clearly slammed down the receiver of the intercom at his end. Frank looked at his side of the intercom, puzzled.

Frank stayed away from the object that he'd fished out of the Pear Drops mixture. He leaned against the metal banister of the staircase leading down to the mezzanine floor, occasionally casting worried glances over to where he'd left it, still in the fishing net on the stone floor by the vat. He puffed out his cheeks in a childish approximation of relief when he saw the lumbering figure of Duckworth turn a corner in the corridor and descend into the boiling room down a ramp. From Frank's vantage point, Duckworth looked a comforting, familiar sight. Not only was he wearing his usual white suit with black pinstripes, his whole body was shaped like an Everton Mint; his torso spread into a roomy oval shape, which tapered off into too-small legs which wobbled like the loose plastic wrapping. Puffing and panting, he made his way across the factory floor towards Frank.

"Ah Frank," he said, "I am delighted at your dedication once again. Here's me thinking we'd be having a quiet night, but you just won't let things go, will you?"

"Uh – are you angry, sir?" said Frank, momentarily nonplussed by his boss's dishevelled state. Up-close, Duckworth seemed to have perfected a just-got-out-of-bed look which was so popular on the TV ads these days. His hair was ruffled up on his crown as though he'd fallen asleep with his head tucked under his arm.

"Angry? Now why would I be angry? Come on; show me this *bone*."

"It's not like a bone that you throw for your dog, sir," said Frank, leading the way to the Pear Drops vat. "They are smaller bones, like the ones you'd imagine were in your fingers…"

"You think it's a human bone?" said Duckworth, suddenly worried again.

"I don't know, sir; all I know is it's got no skin on it and it is bright white like the paint they put in my mother's bathroom."

Indeed, as they stood over the object, they saw that it was indeed startlingly white, like polished ivory. The bones, as they surely were, were collected in a formation which resembled – a foot? There was one large, ball-shaped bone which was loosely connected to a collection of smaller bones – digits? There were only four of these digits; the bones of the feet are generally held together by ligaments, and these had been most likely boiled clean away by the Pear Drops mixture's volcanic temperatures.

Duckworth took one look and a cloud of grey fear began to form across his brows. Frank knelt down and attempted to get a better look; he kept opening and closing one eye and then the other. It was clear that he had no idea what he was looking at.

"Get up, Frank," breathed Duckworth, sounding weak. "This is just a silly hoax; that's all."

"What is it though, sir?" said Frank, looking imploringly at his superior.

"It's a damn prank; that's what. Your friends Marsden and Keen probably put it there; the fools; Halloween's round the corner and they're probably just trying to scare us, that's all."

"No sir; that's a new batch. I opened the pipes to let in some new water at the start of my shift; straight out of the river; fresh."

"You added all the ingredients yourself?"

"Yeah, just like I was told…"

"Don't worry Franky-boy," said Duckworth, patting him on the shoulder. "There's nothing for you to worry about. In fact; why don't you get yourself off home for the night? I'll clean this up."

"But Mr. Duckworth, I want to help," said Frank, before extending his bottom lip in a brilliant impression of a five-year-olds' sulk.

Duckworth chewed over Frank's words as though he'd just bitten through the hard outer shell of a lemon bonbon. His lips pursed in wincing disapproval. "I used to work down here before they sent you down here…"

"When I was on the production line?" said Frank, forgetting he was supposed to be sulking.

"Yeah; that's right. I was supervisor down here when ol' Funnel was around…"

"God rest his soul."

"That's right; but let me continue. Well, in those days, the pipe from the river was much smaller, and we were always getting blockages of some sort or other… I was the only one that went down there to unblock the pipe."

"Is that why they made you boss, boss?"

"Probably, yes," said Duckworth, and the trace of a wicked smile played at the corners of his mouth.

"I can go down there for you, sir."

"Just forget about it for now; if there are any more of these *objects*, let me know," said Duckworth, depositing the bones into a plastic bag and starting to walk away. "And Frank? Make sure that you don't tell anybody else about this. Think of this as a game; our little secret. Can you do that for me?"

And things would have stayed like that, just hanging there, unresolved, had Frank not been the good worker that he was. Maybe everyone else in the factory would have been glad that the episode had been brushed under the carpet, but Frank didn't want there to be any mess anywhere, even if it was hidden from view under the carpet. As Halloween dragged ever closer, fellow workers began to notice a change in their colleague; instead of the inane grin which he usually wore to work, his face was now screwed into a stern mask of concentration. He was thinking.

Frank even began to shun the factory canteen. Instead, he could be found walking up and down the river bank, hands clasped behind his back as though he thought he was Hercule Poirot or someone. The factory was built on top of the river, allowing its pure water to pump into its bowels, where it would be mixed with sugars and powders to make boiled sweets, lollipops, sugary drinks. Frank used to sit at one of the lonely old picnic tables down there and simply stare at the factory as it towered above him like some medieval fortress.

Down by the river, the factory almost sounded as though it was alive. From here, the staple sounds which bound together his each and every day seemed alien and not-quite-right. As the factory belched out its intoxicating, sugary steam, it almost sounded like the wheezy exhalations of an old man; the creaks and the moans made by the machines were like the rumbling tummy of a hungry traveller. Frank watched and listened, and tried to work out where the blockage in the system might be found. His mind worried away at him; what was that scurrying sound which he sometimes heard? It sounded like it was coming from the very depths of the factory; from the very old part which nobody ventured into any more.

And then Frank began to formulate some kind of a plan. He took paper and pencils to the river bank and began sketching what he thought the innards of the factory might look like. He had an untutored hand, but there was a grim determination in his etchings which made them somehow realistic. Frank was going to plumb the depths of the factory and save the taste-buds of the children of the world. He drew himself as some kind of hero, receiving the adulation of a swarming mass of people. He imagined Duckworth smiling from ear to ear and offering him a small box-room in the factory, where he could sleep if he needed to.

He had to get himself back on the night shift; Marsden was working on it now, and Frank shuddered to think about the standard of the sweets which had been turned out over the past couple of weeks. Marsden was a slacker and a drinker. He always looked down his nose at Frank and spoke to him really slowly as though talking to a toddler. At least Keen wouldn't be with him though; that pair were always trying to outdo each other in their pranks and escapades. They seemed to see the factory like it was a playground. Keen wasn't exactly 'Keen by name, keen by nature', as Duckworth used to say. But Keen hadn't been seen for a couple of weeks now. Frank had heard rumours that he'd managed to get himself a maintenance job on a cruise ship or something; well, good riddance to bad rubbish.

Frank had been to see Duckworth about the possibility of being put on the night shift again, but had felt fobbed-off with the response he'd got. He'd been told that Marsden was being put in the boiling room in Halloween week as some kind of punishment for something or other, and that it was for the good of the factory that he remained there. Now, anyone else in the factory would have definitely let go at this point, but Frank did not; he was like a dog with a bone.

One day, he decided to stay late after his shift had finished, and he waited for Marsden to arrive at the changing rooms to get ready for the night shift. Usually, Frank hated the changing rooms and waited until he got home to have his shower – not caring what the world thought of the smell of sweets which clung to him – but on this day, he felt as though it was some kind of a test. He allowed himself to be subjected to the angry towel-whippings from his colleagues, allowed himself to sit there while they pranced around naked and behaved like sniggering school-kids. Then he continued to sit and wait in that cold room until Marsden finally deigned to show up.

But it was a different Marsden which entered the changing room. Gone was the mischievous sparkle in his eyes, replaced by a hollow indifference. He'd stopped gelling his hair; it now resembled a bird's nest which had been haphazardly propped on top of his head. His clothes were dirty, and he smelled of defeat. He almost jumped out of his skin when Frank spoke to him. He'd entered the changing rooms with his head down, as though resigned to his fate.

"Marsden?" said Frank, again.

"What the hell are you still doing here, you retard?" said Marsden gruffly, visibly annoyed by the terror he'd shown when Frank had first spoken to him.

"I'd like to swap shifts with you; will you speak to Mr. Duckworth?" said Frank, crossing his fingers behind his back.

"And why the hell would you want to do that?" said Marsden, approaching Frank with a cold hard look in his eyes.

"I don't feel right in the day-shift…" muttered Frank, suddenly scared of this hulking brute.

"Get out of here Frank," sighed Marsden. "You don't know what you're asking…"

"I do, I do…"

"No, you don't. Are you completely stupid or is it just an act?" said Marsden, gripping the lapels of Frank's suit jacket. His knuckles had turned white. "Did Duckworth send you here to test me?"

"No," squealed Frank, "I came here off my own back. I want to see something…"

"What do you want to see?" said Marsden, loosening his grip somewhat.

"There's things getting into the system, see, and Mr. Duckworth told me that something might be blocked…"

"Did he tell you that?"

"No, I worked it out from what he said. We found bones…"

"You what?" roared Marsden. "Frank; stay away from the night shift. Don't get involved in things that don't concern you. Have you never wondered why they say 'curiosity killed the cat'?"

"I'm only trying to help," said Frank, blinking away the tears. "Why are you shouting at me?"

"So you get it through your thick skull that what happened to Keeno might happen to you if you don't watch yourself. You don't want to be in this place around Halloween, Frank. Don't ask me why. Just take my word for it."

Frank's head was sore from where nasty Marsden had prodded him when he'd been shouting. You should never touch other people, not unless they expressly ask you to; that's what his mother had told him. Marsden's mother clearly hadn't been as thorough in her education of her son. Frank felt a little sorry for big old Marsden, because he'd shown that deep-down he was scared, and *he* had nothing to fall back on; *he* had no kind words to make sense of the world. Now more than ever, Frank was convinced that there was *something* going on at the factory which wasn't right. Why else were all of these signs flashing out at him?

Frank left the changing rooms but he didn't leave the factory. He waited in a gloomy part of the corridor and waited for Marsden to emerge. Sure enough, a few minutes later, a big shadow crept out of the changing room door and shuffled down the corridor towards the boiling room. Taking care not to make a sound, Frank followed him. It helped that Marsden wasn't looking anywhere but at a spot on the floor directly in front of him; he wasn't expecting to be followed.

They crept, in their strange, single-file procession, down into the boiling room, where Marsden began to stagger down the metal stairwell to the mezzanine floor. Frank had to remove his shoes so as not to clatter and jangle the stairs the way that Marsden had. He tucked them safely away under one of the vats and then set off after his colleague, realising that he'd never been down to the mezzanine before. He'd been told that it was out of bounds, and had never questioned this direct order.

Feeling a strange mix of adrenaline, liberation and dread upon him, Frank made it to the foot of the stairs just in time to see Marsden disappear into a narrow, almost-hidden doorway cut into the stone wall on the far side of the room. As the door closed behind him, Frank noted that the door had a large sign on it which read 'Danger: Do Not Enter'. All of his soul cried out that he should not go through that door, but somehow his body pressed on. He touched the cold steel of the door with a trembling hand, and promptly pushed it open; fearing that it's tell-tale creak would alert Marsden to his presence. But the door appeared to be well-oiled, and it swung open without even a whisper of complaint.

The door closed behind him with a sound like the *whump* of a ball hitting a hollow wooden box. Panicked, Frank strained his eyes to check where Marsden was, but he was nowhere to be seen. The whole of the corridor was empty; it was empty of anything. It was the cold, sterile corridor of a mental institution; Frank knew such places. Gritting his teeth, he walked on down the corridor, feeling the cold of the stone floor on his bare feet. And then he heard it; that strange scurrying sound that he sometimes heard when he was on the picnic bench on the riverbank. Only now it was much louder, much more insistent. It sounded like something scurrying to get its food. Frank thought back to the scared, hollow look in Marsden's eyes and suddenly thought that he might have the answer; was there some kind of group of tiny monsters down there? Was Marsden feeding them? Or was he the food?

Taking a deep breath, Frank tried to regain his composure. He wished that he could be anywhere in the world apart from where he was right now. Mostly, he wished that he was standing over the Pear Drops vat that day, and that he had simply ignored the object he'd seen in there. But that object had been trying to tell him something; maybe the object was Keen's foot? Now that Frank thought about it, the object did look alarmingly like the foot of the skeleton in that book which his mother had banned him from reading because it gave him nightmares.

Nightmares! Surely this was just a nightmare; a particularly vivid nightmare, in which things like the cold steel, or the smooth stone under his feet seemed so real that he was actually there; but a nightmare nonetheless. But no, something about the way in which all of the hairs on the back of his neck stood to attention when he heard that new sound told Frank that this was no nightmare. For what he'd heard was the blood-curdling yell of desperation of a man about to be eaten. *Marsden!* Though he disliked the man, surely nobody deserved to be eaten alive?

Frank increased his pace, taking care not to slip on the floor which was now coated in a film of grease, or oil. What was it? He didn't want to look down, knowing that he'd see blood. His thick toes squirmed uncomfortably in the liquid, trying not to touch too much of it, like the man who had walked barefoot into a mound of dog dirt. A wave of nausea coursed through his veins and he pulled up his trouser legs almost unconsciously. It was all very well getting this crap, or blood on his bare feet, but not on his trousers…

Finally the corridor led somewhere; it led to another small door. Unlike the cold steel of the earlier door, this one positively thrummed with heat and energy. Touching it, Frank felt a charge of power leap up his arm, as though he'd received an electric shock. Something wanted to get out of there; something which felt like evil. Something was beyond the door which would do far worse than ruin his trousers. He could hear the tormented yelping of a man in pain.

Again the door was not locked, and it took a simple shove from Frank and he was through it. Through to the other side; he'd crossed the threshold into hell, or so it felt to him. The atmosphere was thick with screams of pain and want. Through tightly clamped eyes, Frank imagined the scenes from his mother's big books; the ones she'd threatened him with when she'd found him doing that monstrous thing under the bed-sheets. He pictured the racks, the bungee rope gallows, and the ever-reaching claws of demons clutching at his body. This was some kind of punishment for disobeying orders, for letting his curiosity take control. This was Halloween's revenge on little boys that had behaved badly.

Gingerly, he opened his eyes again, seeing the heat before he could make out any distinct shapes. The heat was tangible – *hell's burning fires* – hotter even than the vats, if that were possible. He felt the walls and floor melting and becoming pliant to his touch; it was as though the whole place was formed from plasticine. As Frank braved his way forward, he left molten footprints in his wake. He saw that he was in the underbelly of the factory; hell. It was a hell of old creaking machinery that promised unimaginable torture on the body; a hell drowning in sticky liquid and gas. It burned into Frank's lungs, choking him, making it difficult to think.

Somehow, he saw the pipes which reared up from the ground like bewitched serpents, and reached into and through the ceiling; into the vats in the boiling room above. Somehow, he made out the figure of a man in the background; a man who was speaking something in hushed tones, like those one would reserve for comforting a child that was ill. Frank couldn't make out the words, nor could he make out who the man was, for he was close to passing out, which he duly did when the screeching started up again.

Frank didn't know how long he'd been out for. He only recognised that he'd woken up because he felt hot liquid around his crotch; he'd wet himself. Gradually he opened his eyes, expecting to see the disappointed eyes of his mother on him, but instead he saw dark, hollow eyes that he recognised from somewhere else.

"You okay Frank?" said a deep voice from somewhere.

"Who is that?" he asked, groggily. "Where am I?"

"It's Marsden, you retard," said the voice, arrogantly. Frank thought that there was relief in the voice too though; it almost sounded like his mother's when she had been worried about him, but then saw that there was nothing to worry about (which there usually wasn't.)

"Why is the ground moving?" gasped Frank, suddenly aware that the floor he was lying on was actually wriggling, like it was alive.

"Oh man… why did you come down here? You don't want to see this…"

"I can't see anything."

"Well, get up, turn around and walk out the door before you do… there's things in this room that will blow your little mind."

Marsden started to pull Frank to his feet. As Frank moved, he felt the floor move with him, reciprocating every shift of his aching body. He felt the strange, hot substance clinging to the skin of his feet and creeping up his shins, under his trouser legs.

"What is that, on the floor?" he said, trying to brush the stuff from his legs with the sleeve of his jacket. It was starting to burn into his skin now. "It's disgusting!"

"Now stop right there a moment, chief," said Marsden, gripping Frank's shoulders. "You don't have any right to come in here – where you're forbidden to come – and criticise what you see; what you don't understand." Marsden sounded like an angry father who'd perceived some slight on his children which he wasn't about to let go. Frank rubbed at his eyes, finally able to see the overwhelming disappointment on his colleague's face.

"Sorry," said Frank, kicking some of the substance away from him in disgust. "I'll go now." As Frank kicked, he heard a strange scurrying sound, as though the floor was trying to get away from him.

"You've frightened them now; you great oaf," said Marsden, and then he bent down and began stroking the floor. In front of Frank's horrified eyes, the substance leaped up Marsden's arms as though magnetically attracted. "Don't be scared my little babies; the silly man won't try and hurt you any more. Daddy's here to protect you…"

"Who are you talking to?" Frank screamed, unable to contain his fear of the darkness any longer. And this darkness wasn't just his gloomy surroundings, it was a lack of understanding, too; he was lost.

As he watched, the substance on the floor began to form small islands. Liquid ran into other liquid and the molecules combined to form larger globules of the stuff. Gradually, these globules grew still further, the liquid starting to solidify in the great temperatures, until they resembled knee-high jelly babies. Sugary strands hung from the tops of their bodies – their heads? – and looked like hair. They were now semi-solid, but also gelatinously pliant-looking, like they were made from something completely different than everything else in the room. Their form could not be defined by any usual scientific terms now; they looked as though they had been formed from strands of ejaculatory fluid in a bath. In their bubbling faces, he began to pick out eyes, noses and mouths.

"What the hell is going on?" Frank yelped, sweat pouring down his face and seeping saltily into the corners of his mouth.

"Frank; meet my babies. Babies; meet your supper," said Marsden, his face now devoid of any emotion.

"H- h – how are these your babies?" stammered Frank.

"Did that mother of yours never teach you about the birds and the bees? Do you not know what happens to the millions of tiny little sperm when you waste them?" grinned Marsden with a wicked gleam now appearing in his eyes.

"What?" muttered Frank.

"We gave them their own little birthing pools here; the sugary liquid was just like amniotic fluid, keeping them alive. Then we bring them down here, to live."

"D – Does Mr. Duckworth know about this?"

"Why? You gonna tell him? Don't be a fool; of course he knows… look at some of these little beauties…"

And Frank looked; he saw the zebra-stripes which faintly covered a number of the larger looking things. He saw that Duckworth had a lot more to do with it all than simply *knowing* about it. Frank started to cry; great globules of snot and tears ran down his grubby face. It was all too much. As he looked at the floor, he noticed that some of the liquid which had seeped out of him was starting to congeal. Was he creating his own Frankenstein's monsters?

"What would Old Man Funnel say about this?" snivelled Frank, his whole world collapsing around him.

"Why, ask him yourself. Your Daddy's in here somewhere..."

"My – Daddy?"

"Yes, you fool. You were the first of them... the first to make it to the outside world. Tell me; did you never think about why everyone said that sugar flowed through your veins?"

"What about mother?"

"An old cleaner... she knows the truth. Ah, here's Funnel now; eating a bit of Keeno's arm. Keeno was your brother, Frank."

Me and my Shadow

The crowd left the theatre in a buzz of excitement. If you'd have stopped any one of them and asked them about the quality of the performance, they'd have confirmed that it was probably the greatest show that they'd ever seen. They would have waxed lyrical about the skills of the performer and they would have marvelled at how time had flown. One minute they'd been settling themselves in their seats, rustling at popcorn and sweets, the next they'd been almost carried out the door by a wave of exhilaration. But if you'd pressed your happy audience member still further about what they'd seen, you'd have started to be met by blank expressions.

Jim Hunter had seen it all before. He'd watched them emerge like washed-up fish, blinking at the incongruous sunlight outside the theatre. Then, with fishy mouths popping open and closed, they would struggle to suck in a draft of comprehension before finally their faces settled on wonder. The audience would begin to flop around, waiting for some safe net to come pick them up, or a welcoming wave of normality to wash over them. From past experience, Hunter knew that he'd have to watch them all go through this whole fish-out-of-water routine before he could finally approach one of them and politely encourage them to re-learn the English language.

Hunter always picked the most sensible-looking people to interview. Sometimes he'd see the flash of white of a dog-collar, or perhaps the sheen of a well-pressed suit and he'd imagine that now, finally, he'd get the straight answer he was looking for. Unfortunately, the one thing that this random collection of people seemed to have in common was the fact that they all shared the same confused features, that same unwillingness to divulge that they had absolutely no idea what they'd just seen. It was as though they'd been lured into a collective trance for the best part of an hour, or that they'd been rudely awakened from some beautiful dream. Hunter was reminded of the tale of The Emperor's New Clothes. Nobody wanted to admit their ignorance.

Jim Hunter had an inbuilt mistrust of shows like this. He didn't allow magic, or even the idea of magic, any credence in his black and white world. There was no such thing as a real vanishing act, no such thing as spontaneous combustion. It was bound to be some trick of the light, some hidden trap-door in the stage, or some new combination of smoke and mirrors. Maybe it was a case of mass hypnosis. That would certainly explain their confused, white-washed faces at the exit. Whatever it was, he didn't believe any aspect of Shadowman's act was true. And what's more, he hated the way in which the man was gulling the general public. Some of the people in attendance were clearly very poor, but had been tricked into parting with their money for something which was a fake.

And so he waited outside the stage door once more to see whether the Shadowman would finally emerge. Yes, he had to admit that it was pretty neat that the guy was never physically seen to leave the theatre after a performance, but again, there'd probably be a rational explanation for that too. The Shadowman probably disguised himself as one of the audience members and left the theatre at exactly the same time they all did. But while there was a chance that Hunter might catch him sneaking out of the back-door, he stayed to wait for him.

The usual crowd waited with him; giggly schoolgirls, excited gangs of lads, shadowy looking disciples of the great man.

"Here again, Hunter?" asked one of these disciples, a tall, crooked-looking man who wore a wide-brimmed hat which hid most of his face.

"Yeah," sighed Hunter. "Some day, he won't slip through my fingers. Someday, I'll catch him."

"But why?" whined the disciple. "Why can't people like you leave him alone?"

"He still has a crime to answer for. You know that as well as I."

The disciple smiled. Like the rest of his body, his mouth was crooked: evil, perhaps. "Ah, but you know as well as I that you can't try a shadow for a crime!"

"You really believe that he is a shadow and not a man? That he can just disappear into thin air when the lights go low?" asked Hunter.

The low hum of the crowd suddenly stopped. Hunter realised that most of the other disciples had started to gather menacingly close around the two of them. The disciples didn't like what he was saying and they especially didn't like the way that he was saying it. Hunter's big, brash policeman's confidence was too obviously out of place in this liminal world where strangeness was a gift, not a crime.

"Why don't you ever go in to see the show?" asked a teenaged girl who had been pushed to the front of the crowd. She had hooded eyes and a massive under-bite. Her chin jutted out at him aggressively.

"Ha!" Hunter tried to laugh, hearing the fear in his own voice. "A fool and his money are easily parted. I'm quite happy waiting for him out here."

"It's because you're scared of him, isn't it?" snarled the girl. She was clearly some kind of ring-leader out here amongst the garbage bins and the discarded stage props. "You let him get away last time and you're scared that you'll let him do it again. Look at you with your big body. You can't get it through your thick skull that there are more things in this world than simple flesh and blood." Hunter took an uneasy step backwards. The girl reminded him of one of those religious zealots that you always saw on the news in the aftermath of some disaster. She was the kind of person that was capable of just about anything in the name of her lord and master. When people have seen the light, it is very difficult to convince them that the light they saw had more to do with electromagnetic radiation than miracle.

"Why do you wait out here when you know that he won't come out?" asked Hunter, trying a new tactic. But still the crowd closed in on him. They were menacingly quiet, almost like shadows themselves.

'Why do you wait?' he repeated, trying to stop the nervousness from creeping into his voice.

"We're protecting him!" shouted the girl defiantly. 'We're a human shield.'

If only she knew, thought Hunter. If only she knew what that man was capable of. Then they wouldn't be out here with their misguided ideas of protection. They'd be the ones that would need protecting.

The Shadowman made his name on the touring circuit. He dragged himself up from the dingy basement clubs and their low-lights, at first supporting more famous hypnotists and illusionists, until he eventually gained his own cult following and began to take centre stage. The spotlights shone brightly on him.

It would be hard to pinpoint the exact reason for his popularity. After all, an air of threat surrounded his performances, an air of shadowy otherness. But some people like that kind of thing; you're never more alive than when you are scared out of your wits. And, of course, Shadowman's shows were more about horror than wonder. Instead of pulling rabbits out of hats, he was skinning them alive, then wearing the fur on his head and then making the poor creature disappear in a puff of smoke or down his shadowy sleeves.

Shadowman seemed to suck his audience into a murky underworld where nothing was quite as it appeared. His trick was to make you convinced that what was solid and real was actually an apparition, and what was shadowy and artificial, as genuine as flesh and blood. Apparently, he convinced some of his followers that they could escape their bodies.

His reputation for the darker side of magic was reinforced when he was linked to a terrible incident at one of his shows; a volunteer from the audience had been decapitated in some stunt which had gone badly wrong. There were rumours that she'd actually laughed, and shouted 'I'm free', before her head was removed. Hunter, who had had been called in as the investigating officer, had expected an open and shut case, but nothing could have been further from the truth. Nobody in the crowd could explain what had happened. All of the usual stage-hands hadn't even been working. Despite the woman's death occurring in front of more witnesses than he'd ever been able to call upon, he hadn't even managed to fill a page of his notebook with their descriptions of what had happened.

Hunter remembered meeting Shadowman's manager as though it had been yesterday. They met in the gloomy theatre ticket office, Hunter expecting much wringing of hands on the part of the manager – his show was, after all, in danger of being cancelled. The manager was a shady, moustachioed man with the air of a circus ringmaster about him. He didn't seem in the least bit perturbed by what had happened.

"But there's no such person as the Shadowman! I would have though that much is obvious," the manager said. "He's a trick of the light and shadows… a non-person. There is no body that you can finger for the crime."

"Well, somebody's to blame for all of this – that poor woman can't go unavenged," Hunter muttered.

"I've told you; you can't arrest a shadow," the manager laughed. Laughed! "There's no body there. It was just a dreadful accident."

And so, Hunter was left clutching at shadows. Nobody took responsibility for the accident at the show – after all, you can't very well hold a dagger of light to blame for a woman's death. Something strange, almost inexplicable had taken place, and no matter how hard he'd tried, he couldn't pin the crime, if that was what it was, on anybody. When the woman's family had been paid off, the investigation had stalled somewhat.

Shadowman's career however, had not stalled. News of the incident had spread like wild-fire and now even more people flocked to see whether this man of the shadows could be real. They were intoxicated by the air of something which smelled remarkably like evil. And finally now, the Shadowman had come back to Hunter's town, and Hunter was determined to find out his trick. Posters about town heralded the return of the 'Real Shadowman: A man of flesh and blood and shadows.'

The picture accompanying the text showed a dark figure under a bright spot-light. You couldn't make out any features on the face apart from a wide, gleaming smile.

As soon as Hunter had seen the posters, he'd known beyond all reasonable doubt that the Shadowman was a real person, and that he was mocking him. Oh, he had theories now too. Maybe the Shadowman was actually the shady manager. He'd certainly seemed somehow unreal and difficult to pin down. Of course, maybe he was someone else; a person who'd always remained in the shadows. What was clear was that Hunter wasn't about to let him get away this time, no matter how many times he had to wait outside his circus of a performance.

And then finally, Jim Hunter decided to pay to watch the man's show. It was a cold, rainy day, and frankly, he was absolutely sick and tired of waiting around outside. He felt a real wrench when he parted with his money for the ticket, but ushered forward by the rest of the crowd, he almost didn't have any choice. He was swept forward, through the vast double-doors which were decorated as though they were the gates of hell, and finally he entered the realm of the Shadowman.

What struck him first was the fact that the rest of the audience began settling meekly, like sheep, into their moth-bitten satin theatre seats. Nobody spoke. Nobody moved a muscle. They were the most polite, most reverent audience he'd ever been a part of. It was almost like being in church.

Then came the dry-ice, pumped through pipes at the side of the stage. Slowly, Hunter felt the deep throb of a thundering bass-line start to play, as though it was emanating from under his feet, from the very bowels of hell. He felt the heady concoction of fear and tension in the atmosphere. It was underscored by the deep will of the people for something magical to occur. They were hungry for spectacle.

And just as this tidal wave of emotion was about to crash, the Shadowman appeared. A wispy figure draped in a long black cloak, to Hunter he looked like a child dressing up as an undertaker. To the rest of the audience he looked like a tiny devil.

"I am Shadowman," he wheezed, sounding as though he was struggling to cope with the thick hellish air. "And I'd like to apologise if I sound a little sad, but it's my body, you see, I really miss him."

Suddenly, the deep throbbing bass-line changed to a jaunty piano tune; 'Me and my shadow'. Hunter had to clamp his fist in his mouth to stop himself from laughing. The tiny creature was silhouetted on a great sheet which descended from the rafters. He was tap-dancing in front of the spotlights in an almost tragic imitation of what would pass for entertainment.

"I am a twin, you see," continued the little figure, finally ending his strange dance. "But my brother is long-gone. All that we have left now is my shadow. Tell me; who wants to come up onto the stage and play the part of my body."

Disbelieving the evidence of his own eyes, Jim Hunter saw that he'd raised his hand high into the air. As though in a trance, he felt himself get up from his seat and begin to walk down from the stalls and onto the stage. He felt as though he was gliding above the plush carpet.

In front of him, on stage, stood what looked like a ghost; it was certainly not a solid form. All around him, Hunter could smell a musty aroma. It was almost exactly what a shadow would smell like. He willed his legs to walk him off the stage, but instead, he saw the wispy figure draw a dagger from under his cloak. As though watching somebody else,

Hunter noticed that he too had drawn one from his own coat. He'd not even known that he had a knife.

Slowly, the shadowy figure lifted the knife to his ghostly neck. Jim Hunter's knife repeated the gesture on his own heavily stubbled neck. The shadow began to cut; Jim Hunter began to cut. As the blood started to pour from his wound, Hunter broke from his reverie. As for the Shadowman, he just disappeared into the shadows.

A.J Kirby

The Sticky End of the Wrong

It was pretty damn easy to get hold of the wrong end of the stick if you ask me. Hell, I know that in the end, I couldn't have got hold of a wronger end of any stick if I'd have grabbed the damn pointy end of a spear, but them's the breaks, my friend. I've always been a little hot-headed; 'angry bear' is what the old boys in the football team used to call me, but I've said it before and I'll say it again. If any of you had seen that damn photograph, you'd have jumped to the same conclusions.

I blame the internet. Never before has it been so easy for any Tom or Harry to become their very own Private Dick. And I ain't excluding myself from that either; I checked up on my own girl as much as the next man. I could see who she'd been communicating with, and when, and even what she'd said to them right up there on my computer screen. I could see which of them young randy bullocks she'd been invited out to meet, and where. And I put a damn stop to it, that's what I did.

Anyways, many was the row we had over who she 'socially networked' with. In the end, I had to limit her to only going on that site when I was present, just to be on the safe side. It was like I imposed this 'parental control' thing on her so she couldn't just go ahead and indulge that darker, saucier side of her personality; you know the side I mean. You'll have seen it in your own women too. It's that flicker of a smile when that ad for talcum powder comes on the idiot box. The one where the buff tennis player steps off-court and is suddenly in the buff in the locker room. Sure, you only see his dimpled bottom, but it's virtually pornography, ain't it? He don't have no shower or nothing; just applies that dandruff stuff all over his feet and then goes outside to sign his autograph for the slavering mob.

A woman's dark side is the side of her that she don't let you see. It's the side that watches *Sex in the City* (or 'Sex up the Shitter' as I call it) and wants to be that tart in it. It's the side that goes off shopping with her pals and talks about cock-size from the minute she sets foot out the house. They're *obsessed*, I tell you. Obsessed. Secretly, all of them want to be dominated by this big alpha male that don't give a shit about them and makes them run around doing the washing up. All this talk of wanting partners that they can share things with is exactly that. Talk.

So, knowing what I know, when I found that photograph, I couldn't think anything other than the fact that it was *incriminating*. It was evidence; that was what it was. One of her friends had put it up on her site, but had 'tagged' Marie. That was how I got to see it, otherwise it would have lain there, rotting through the internet wires or whatever it is, *laughing* at me and my mind-blowing stupidity. As it was, I got to see it, and the last laugh will be mine.

I didn't think anything could shock me any more until I saw that photograph. I thought I'd seen it all. Back in my teens, before the baby came along, I partied with the best of 'em. I went to more of them sex shows than you could shake your damn stick at. So you'll forgive me for getting hold the wrong end of it. What I saw was tantamount to a signed confession from Marie that she'd done the dirty on me, and what's more, she was pleased with herself for doing it. She was revelling in the fact that she was rubbing my face in the crap.

She's got this lunatic, not-a-care-in-the-world grin on her face. It's like a magnification of all of those little flickery smiles into something bigger, more repulsive. You can see the sheen of excited sweat on her forehead and her dancing eyes. She looks kinda hyper-alive. Her dress is fair falling open at the front, and anyone that happened to be standing, leaning over her, would be treated to a full-on view of what lay underneath.

As it happens, there is a man standing over her, and no doubt he's enjoying his eyeful. The man is another of those buff tennis-types. Probably got some slick name like Rick or Dave. Has muscles muscling in on muscles. You know the type. The type that likes to parade around the locker room *wanting* you to raise your eyes. Hell, you don't even need to raise your eyes with some of those fuckers. Their dicks swing at eye-level anyway. Great meaty chunky things, the thickness of a can of coke, banging against their thighs like baseball bats. These men stay naked as long as they possibly can, while you sneak, towel wrapped round your waist, to the showers. Like any normal, decent human being that isn't caught up in trying to get other men aroused or anything like that.

Rick or Dave, or whoever he is, is standing over Marie on some kind of a stage. No; it *is* a stage. The girls are at some kind of seedy strip club. One of them has placed her bottle of Pink Fire right there on the edge of the stage. Rick or Dave could probably kick it over if he wanted to. But he hasn't yet. He's more interested in this 'meeting of minds' with my Marie. From what I can see on the picture, it's like both of them have forgotten they are in this room full of the dregs of humanity and instead believe that they are alone on some picturesque beach like in some of those old flicks I used to record on the old VCR. Rick or Dave is flexing his muscles, all greased up like he's about to perform the 'greatest stunt in the world'; climbing back up his own slimy arse-hole. But, despite the fact that he's semi-naked, gyrating in front of my girl, saucing her up, the one thing that you can't avoid noticing about this A-Grade loser is his eyes.

His eyes look as though they are on fire. Of course, everyone and their dog knows that camera flashes sometimes cause red-eye, but if that's the case then why only *his* eyes? Some say that the eyes are the gateway to the soul, or some such nonsense, but if that it's the case with Rick-Dave, then he is the mother-fucking devil incarnate. His soul burns like red hell. It burns so brightly that even when I've turned the computer screen off and walked mindlessly into the kitchen for a beer, I can still see those eyes tattooed onto the backs of my own eyelids. Marie has unleashed this kinda burning desire in him which can't mean anything else but he's going to fuck her all the ways possible outside in his over-sized car with his over-sized cock and his over-sized ignorance of me, on my way to find him.

Of course I asked Marie about the picture. As soon as I did, she flinched, like I was about to knock ten-bells out of her. But I wasn't that stupid; I wouldn't do anything of the sort until she gave her testimony. *Then* I'd launch into my own unique brand of justice. I was impressed though, with the restraint that I showed. It went something like this:

ME: *(Polite to the nth degree)* 'Dearest; I'd like to ask you a personal question?'

HER; THE ADULTERESS; THE COCKSUCKING QUEEN OF SLEASE; THE WOMAN WHO CAN'T SAY NO; THE DISEASE-RIDDEN WHORE: What the fuck you want now, Bill? Cain't you see that I'm watching the shopping channel and

spending all your hard earned money on gear that will make me look like a hooker next time I go out with the girls…
ME: *(softly, soothingly)* I don't like it when you go out with the girls. I like spending time with you, talking about hopes and dreams and looking after Mikey.
THE DEVIL'S SPUNK-BUCKET: I can't be bothered with Mikey, Bill. Cain't you look out for him again? Anyway, what was your pathetic little question?
ME: I… I just wondered what you were doing on that photograph of you on that website…
THE CUNT: WHAT THE HELL YOU DOING SPYING ON ME YOU DIRTY BASTARD? You ain't got no right to do that…
ME: Oh, Marie; what have you done to me? To us?
THE CUNT: I ain't done nothin'. That picture shows nothin'. We was out for Charlotte's Hen Party and I jus' got dragged along. I never even looked at the man, just hung back and had a few Pink Fires. That picture's got me all wrong. The camera *can* lie, you know. Or is that beyond your meagre intell-i-gence to understand?

Marie remained tight-lipped over the whole thing. Which is more than can probably be said for her on the night in question. But I took the fact that she must have got Charlotte to take the picture down off the site as an indication of her guilt in the matter. And I couldn't forget about it, even after I tired of hitting her, or going out and taking out my frustrations on the street-girls off Main.

I remember it hitting me that I had to do something about it after I failed to climax with this gap-toothed monstrosity in the bin-store out back of Lieutenant Bob's burger joint. I just zipped up, flung some loose change at her and headed straight back to the house. Marie was sat up, staring vacantly at some shitty television programme. She was so withdrawn these days that she'd even let little Mikey stay up way beyond his bedtime. Maybe she was pining for her devil.

Anyways, so I got to thinking that I'd try to find out some more about that swarthy character at the strip club. I'd find out if he was a regular there, or whether he was like some travelling cocksman that got his kicks from going into little communities like ours and messing up all of the God-fearing marriages which lay within. Charlotte, who was now married to Glen from the Gas Station, was my best bet. I knew Glen from the old days – football – and could rely on a bit of his male solidarity to get Charlotte to give me the answers I was looking for.

"They went down The Banana and Two Plums, Bear," said Glen. He was still, I noticed, using my Angry Bear nickname after all these years. Maybe while Marie pined for her devil and I pined for the truth, old Glen pined for the old days. Marriage can do that to good folk. It can climb in your bed in the dead of night and suck out all your enthusiasm like some devilish vacuum cleaner. Glen looked tired. He could hardly hold himself upright, leaning back against the bonnet of my shining Sarcophagus and talking in this slow drawl which made him seem kinda stupid, which I knew he wasn't.

"Where that?" I said, spitting out some of the remaining tobacco leaves which Glen had offered me. It wasn't chewing tobacco, but was just the stuff from a cigarette. Glen couldn't smoke down by the pumps and this, he told me, was the next best thing. See what I mean about him not being as stupid as he sounded?

"Bout twenny mile down toward the border, six past the big Lieutenant Bob's on the Highway," droned Glen. I'd forgotten that he always measured distances by way of how close places were to a Lieutenant Bob's.

I hopped straight in the Sarcophagus and high-tailed it for the Highway, forgetting, in my haste, to pay for my gas. Well; old Glen knew I was good for it, didn't he?

The Banana looked abandoned, like there hadn't been anyone there for years. The surrounding forest looked as though it needed little more time before it reclaimed the place as its own once more. You could hardly picture hoards of screaming women hot for blood inside, and itching with sin in the queue outside. It was a low-slung concrete building with a corrugated iron roof in some places. It looked more like a shack in the Dominican Republic than some entertainment venue. The car park was more like a dust-bowl. In fact, the only sign of the place's former life was the old neon sign – half of the word 'Banana' was now missing so it read

'The Ban and Two Plums' – and the smell. The whole place stunk of sex. A fishy, salty, *forbidden* aroma clung to everything. It was as though some mad magician somewhere had tried to concoct *the* smell of seediness. If you bottled it up, you could truly sell a perfume called Sex which would put all of the other imitators out of business.

I got out of the car and slunk over to the building. For some reason, maybe it was the smell, maybe something else; this unfamiliar feeling of dread was creeping up on me. I kept expecting that at any moment, Rick or Dave or Satan would come flying out of the boarded-up windows and attack me while I was unprepared, while I hadn't got my fighting head on. And another thing. There was this funny little voice which kept butting into my chain of thoughts. It kept saying things like: *you were joking before about that stripper being the devil, but out here, in amongst the closely packed trees, you're starting to believe, aren't you? Out here, the man with the cloven hooves and the horns might very well exist. And he's probably right at home in a place like this.*

I tried to put the annoying voice out of my mind. I tried to concentrate on the task in hand. I was here to find Mr. I've-Fucked-Your-Wife, and this was where he was last seen. The old me would have taken some kind of perverse pleasure in the fact that the man had been reduced to entertaining a pack of hags like Charlotte's gang at a spot as dilapidated as this. You don't really get any lower in terms of the show-business ladder.

I walked on. Although it was only early evening, darkness was already setting in. I'd forgotten how far out in the sticks the place actually was; there was very little in the way of artificial light to help me out. I almost jumped out of my skin when I heard some animal make this almighty howl from the dark fir trees.

Collecting myself again, I moved forward and placed a trembling hand on the cold concrete as I tried to peer through a crack in the boards on the window. I don't know what I was expecting to see, but when my eyes became accustomed to the dark, I took in the view of the interior of The Banana with some confusion. Just like the outside of the building, the inside looked as though nobody had been there for years. Dust covered everything, as did the droppings of a number of animals. It also looked as though the place had been left in a hurry; cracked old chairs lay upended, broken tables wobbled three-leggedly as though they had been halted mid-dash as they tried to escape out the door. In fact, the whole place looked as though it had been covered in volcanic ash, forever frozen in one, long-passed moment in time like that place in Europe, Pom Pay.

I moved away from the window and stalked round the building, heading for the doorway. I'd avoided it at first because unfriendly metal shutters had been closed over the whole thing. *Rather like closing away a tomb* said that strange voice in my head. I told it to shut the hell up and went about my business. If there was anyone watching; if there were any eyes in that thick, dank forest, they must have reckoned me a loon. Most folk do if they see a fella talking to himself.

Anyways, as I approached the doorway, I saw that it was flanked by these two large pillars, on the sides of which were these old tattered posters advertising the male strippers. I leaned in to take a closer look. It was strange; the men on the posters looked as though they were throwbacks to a bygone age. Most of them had these long, thin ringmaster moustaches and were wearing these old-style all-in-one striped bathing suits. It didn't look like any kinda male strip show I'd ever seen. Not that I frequent that kinda event, but you know what I mean. They weren't like the men you see on the internet, and they certainly weren't like Rick or Dave. Or Satan.

Without any clear idea of why I was doing it, I started to bang on the metal shutters. I do things like that sometimes. I'm a spur of the moment kinda guy.

"Oi!" I yelled. "Is there anybody in there?"

I felt a little stupid yelling at a clearly empty building, but this felt like the kinda place where weird stuff just happens so I behaved accordingly. Part of me got to thinking that maybe it was all some kind of hidden camera trick show and that the host would emerge from the forest, all-smiles, and talk in front of the whole damn nation about what a damn fool I was. But nothing like that happened. Something far stranger happened, in fact.

This small letterbox thing – I'd not noticed it before despite the fact it was right in the middle of the metal shutter - suddenly creaked open. I took a step back. I could hear that little voice in my head again, saying something like: *you better run for it now, boy, before it too late. You know what curiosity did?*

Then a real voice spoke, and this was far more worrying than the fact that some strange yokel was preaching in my head. "What you want?" it said, gruffly.

When I first tried to speak, I felt as though my throat was going to close right up. My words came out this strangled, pathetic whine. I took a deep breath and tried again.

"I'm... uh... looking to speak to someone about a male stripper."

The voice gave this low grumble. It sounded like a clap of thunder. I realised that it was laughing. "You don't look the type," it said, finally.

I tried to peer into the thick blackness through the letterbox, tried to see if I could see those fiery read eyes. For as soon as I did, I was outta there, no matter how much of a yellow-belly it made me... I saw nothing.

"Well," said the voice, "are you the type? You like lookin' at other men?"

"No. No I don't. Look, I think I got the wrong place. I think someone's playin' some cruel trick on me sending me here." I rubbed my hand over my stubbled chin, trying to look more nonchalant than I felt.

I started to walk away. The voice stopped me in my tracks.

"I don't think Marie or Charlotte have the... *creativity* to come up with something like that, do you?" it asked.

"How do you... who are you? Is this..." The questions poured out of me like some goddam fountain or something. I swear that whoever owned the voice was probably enjoying watching me squirm. Whoever it was knew about my worst nightmares and was playing on them.

"Wanna come in? Shoot the breeze some more?" asked the voice, more playfully this time. They were in a position of power and they knew it. "It's gonna get dark soon, and you don't wanna be out there when that happens."

"Why? What happens then?" I couldn't stop myself from talking. I was becoming a woman.

"The real question you should be asking, my friend, is whether you are dressed suitably enough to gain entry to this establishment. Usually, we have a very strict dress code."

And then the voice roared with laughter again. I looked down at myself. Over my rapidly expanding paunch I could see my old faded denim shorts and my flip-flops for what they really were; sad attempts to hold on to my youth. My T-Shirt, which bore the legend 'X-Rated Show Downstairs' with an arrow pointing toward my crotch, was simply asking for trouble.

The metal shutter groaned loudly and then began to roll upwards. For a terrifying moment, I thought I was going to lose control over my bladder. When the moment was over, I took another step backwards and steeled myself for what I was about to see.

In the gloom behind the door stood an average man of average height, average weight and indeterminate age. He wasn't rippling with muscles, but neither was he someone that I was sure of beating if it came down to a brawl. There was something attractive about the man. About his personality, I mean. And he looked as regular as one of the guys I see down at the bar. And come to think of it, he did have a glass full of clear, slightly sparkling liquid which he held out to me. It looked as though someone had dropped a plink-fizz pill in it or something.

"Go on, take it," said the man, smiling. His voice was now far less powerful. It was as though the amplification lent to it by the metal shutters had now gone away and he had been unmasked as just a run of the mill guy, like you and me. The only thing strange about him was the fact that he was wearing sunglasses at this time of night, and inside, to boot. Who did he think he was? Some kinda rock star?

"It ain't drugged, if that what you thinkin'," he said, merrily, before his body collapsed into a ragged bout of coughing. I took the glass from him before he spilled any more of it. I sniffed; the faint aroma of something lemony wafted into my nostrils; something sour in there too. It smelled a little bit like Marie does after a night on the Pink Fire.

"It's gin and tonic," he continued. "Got quinine in it; keeps the damn mozzies off. They can plague you out here this time of year."

To save face, or perhaps just for something to do, seeing as though I still seemed unable to make head nor tail of the situation, I took a long gulp. It was wonderful; just the right mix of refreshing tartness and alcoholic kick. I took another slug, like I was drinking beer.

"Whoah there soldier," said the man. "Save some for later. The mozzies flock in here later on. They seem to like the smell of the place."

"Smells like sex," I said, somewhat woozily. The booze was already going to my head a little. I never was a spirits man. I've always held that they are more for women or people that's scared of that bloated feeling, like drowning, that you get sometimes when you have over nine pints.

"Or death," remarked the man. He regarded me cryptically; maybe I was swaying a little. I certainly felt like I was.

"Who are you?" I asked, taking advantage of my tipsiness to ask the killer question.

"Oh, we'll get to that," he said. Then, without another word, he turned his back, collected this walking stick from behind the door and tottered away down this little corridor away from the doorway. The stick was made of wood, but had this heavy-looking handle which was shaped like a horses head. Each step that he took was accompanied by the staccato *tap-tap* of this stick on the wooden floor. Weirdly, it sounded like what dancing high heels sound like. Eventually I followed after him, creaking over the rotten floorboards wondering what the hell was going on.

The stage door opened with an audible sigh as though it hadn't been opened in years. I could hardly breathe, such was the thickness of the cloud of dust which we disturbed as the door opened. We both stood back and surveyed the wreckage of the former strip club. The average man had his hands behind his back, kinda like he was proud of the place and was waiting for me to throw in some suitable complements and whatnot.

"What happened here?" I said.

"You like your questions, Mr. Dawkins," commented the average man.

"How do you…"

"I've just the thing that'll cheer you up though," he interrupted. "I'll put on a little music."

The average man limped over to the corner of the stage where there was a dustsheet covering something or other. He whipped the sheet away like he was one of those television magicians pulling out the table-cloth but keeping all the crockery and plates on the table. Underneath was this old-style record player. He lifted the plastic cover and placed the needle on a record which was already on the turntable. A loud crackly sound reverberated around the room and finally some tinny 80's music started up. Funny thing about the record player was the fact that I couldn't see no wires coming off it. It wasn't plugged into anything at all. Being a technical kinda guy, I notice shit like that.

Anyways, I had no time to think about the ramifications of this; the average man was lumbering back to where I was stood. As he trundled, he performed this strange kinda wiggle like he was getting into the music. He waved his stick about almost as though he was conducting an orchestra or something. This mad-as-a-coot place was becoming stranger by the minute.

"Know this number?" asked the average man. He had to raise his voice a little to be heard over the spooky music. I simply shook my head by way of an answer.

"It's 'Goodbye Horses' by Q. Lazarus. Pop classic. You'll have heard it all before. Seen the film *Silence of the Lambs*?"

Suddenly I *did* recognise the tune. It was the number that was playing when that crazy-ass Buffalo Bill character dressed himself up as a tranny, tucking his own little number between his legs.

"It puts the lotion in the basket," I answered, quoting from the film. I'd watched that part over and over again. There was something so affecting about that whole scene.

"It *does* put the lotion in the basket, doesn't it? So anyway, Mr. Dawkins, you'll be wondering why I brought you here, hmmm?"

I hated the way he asked a question by making a statement and then putting an 'hmmm' at the end of it. It reminded me of this nasty little English teacher we had at school way back when. That bitch hated the very bones of me. Anyway, I say that just to explain why, when I answered the man, I spoke in such a flippant, probably unwise way.

"You never brought me here, chief. My old Sarcophagus brought me here. Old Glen down at the Gas Station gave me directions."

"Fair enough. If that's the way you wanna play it, well, that's fine by me. Now, I have to ask before I do it; which way you wanna go?"

"Which way?"

The average man sighed and flipped away a fat mozzie that was floating around his head like a miniature hot air balloon. "How wouldja like me to kill you?"

The glass of gin and tonic slipped from my fingers and in slow motion descended to the floor. When it hit, I had time to watch each and every fragment shatter off in different directions. The liquid puddled on the floor by my boots.

"I don't usually ask," continued the average man, "but you seemed to be doing such a good job of being bad that I felt I'd give you a bit of extra time and show you the courtesy of asking."

"Who are you?" I whimpered. I suddenly realised that I could feel a patch of dampness around my groin. I had now, finally, pissed myself. Funny that I'd only had half a glass of gin and tonic to achieve that feat; it usually takes me at least eight or nine beers.

"Aw, come on Mr. Dawkins; you know who I am. You've always known."

"The devil," I moaned.

"Some may call me that," he admitted. Slowly, he removed his sunglasses. Mad red eyes stared back at me. "But that's not important right now…"

"But when you saw Marie, you were some kinda male stripper," I gasped. "And you didn't kill her…"

"Basically, Bill; may I call you Bill? Basically, I make you see what you want to see. Marie wanted to see the horny old devil, so I gave it to her. *Course* I didn't kill her though Bill. I just wanted to get your juices goin' so you'd come on all the way out here. And, as you might have guessed, I look kinda different for you. I didn't know you liked guys, Bill?"

"I don't… you're playin' some kinda trick…"

"That's what I like about you, Bill," laughed the average Satan, clapping me hard on the back, "you're always getting hold of the wrong end of the stick."

When he said stick, he suddenly lifted up his walking stick with the metal horse-head handle and he drove it directly into my skull. As I died, he left a long, lingering kiss on my lips. For once in my whole goddam miserable life, I was happy. The mozzies started to dance around me, lapping up the spilled blood like they were in some kinda nightclub and it was the booze. They knew what was good for them, the mozzies; I had to give them that.

The Allotment

I can still hear myself, pregnant with self-importance, saying to you: "all these women do is toss a handful of meaningless platitudes into the wind and wait for them to land on the fertile ground of the hopelessly hopeful." God; how I must have sounded like a bitter, self-important old man.

Is this what getting old does to you? Does it suck your goodness out of you and replace it with the sour fruit of unjust defeat? Maybe I'm making excuses for myself, but it hit me hard, you know, when they let me go. I had to have something… someone in my life that I could *beat*. And so I used to look down on you for holding on to little shoots of hope like the mediums.

I thought it was sick, Margaret, the way that they preyed on people who were grieving. And in a way, I felt like I was losing you, too. The mediums took you away from me, and into a world that I did not know; could not know. That's why you'd always find me hanging around just outside the doors. That's why I didn't 'just go out, then' if I 'hated it so much.' I wanted to hear what nonsense was infecting your brain, just like when I peek over the top of my newspaper at your soap operas and cooking shows. And then, of course, I'd be able to make your life a misery by ridiculing whatever you held dear.

The medium was sitting at our kitchen table nursing a steaming cup of tea. She looked a little perplexed; had she foreseen my arrival? I fixed her with one of my best disbelieving looks and pulled out the chair opposite her. She was a small, sweet-looking old woman with curly hair that had been dyed bright red for effect. I say 'old woman', but now I come to think of it, she was probably about our age, wasn't she? We're probably of the age now where you could, if you so chose, have your hair coloured red or blue, just like the kids which hang around outside the Corn Exchange.

"You're sceptical," she said. Not asking; telling. She was braver than she looked.

"I've had a few women like you in my house, and I want to know exactly what kind of lies you've been filling my wife's head with," I said, leaning forward across the table a little aggressively, I'm afraid.

"You're scared of what she might learn," said the woman, not flinching.

"Nonsense. Alright then, let's get on with it; where's your crystal ball?"

"It doesn't work like that," said the tiny woman in a voice which, I could have sworn, bore traces of an Irish accent. "Give me your hand."

My hand remained resolutely clamped to the side of the kitchen table. I saw that my knuckles were turning white such was the force of my self-righteous indignation.

She reached across the table and gently stroked at the top of my hand and then a concerned look crossed her face.

"You've lost something precious," she said. "But you will find it again, somewhere you least expect."

And there it was; the sum total of her wisdom: utter meaningless platitude. After all, everyone's lost *something* haven't they, even if it's just a pet dog or a credit card? I felt like laughing in her face. I'd been proven right.

"Is that all you've got for me?" I asked, grinning like a loon. But she kept on stroking my hand, ignoring my rudeness.

"The loss has struck deeply into your heart. Nothing can grow there now."

"You're not talking about my bloody job, are you?" I asked, incredulous.

Everyone has to retire. I started to pull my hand away, but then realised that I couldn't. It was as though it had been nailed to the kitchen table, or turned to stone. I felt a flicker of doubt pass through me; just a flicker, but it was enough.

"It isn't a job that you're looking for, is it?" asked the woman with a faint smile. She knew my predicament; she knew that she had me trapped. I avoided her eyes, which were x-raying into my mind.

"No," I managed to whimper. "It's not the job… what the hell have you done to me?"

She didn't speak, but somehow, I heard her words reverberating through my head: *find what you have lost. Before it's too late.*

"Too late?" I stammered, before realising that I'd actually acknowledged the strange voice in my head, even though I hadn't wanted to.

"Why do the vegetables in your allotment not grow?" she asked.

"How… how did you know about that?" I said, feeling myself growing a little faint.

"You plant the seeds but everything withers away and dies, doesn't it? You buy carrots and onions from the supermarket sometimes on your way home and give them to your wife. You don't tell her about the barren nature of your soul."

"Leave me alone," I cried.

"I told you; don't worry. You will find it again," she said, and this time the lilting Irish accent was unmistakeable. "You'll find it where you least expect it."

Gradually, and for no earthly reason I can think of, I began to feel mightily soothed. It's like she saw my loss frozen into the furrows on my brow; when she touched my hand, I felt electricity flowing through her. I don't really know how to put it, but it was as though I took some of this energy into myself, like in the allotments where the tomatoes come up much better if they've been near the peas. Or rather, it's like in my father's allotment, not my own strangled mess of weeds.

When she left, my hand was still resting, palm-down on the kitchen table. It was shaking with a mixture of fear and a left-over electric charge from the woman's own hand. My long, slender fingers – pianists' hands, you always used to say – looked strangely alien to me. I didn't recognise those mottled liver spots, which have suddenly sprung up like spores of bacteria. I didn't recognise the mangled mess of the fingernails. Fingernails which for some unaccountable reason, I've now taken to worrying-away at with my teeth after years of care and attention. Most of all, my ring-finger seems unreal. The skin there is still of a different hue to the rest of my hand. It is newer, pinker, where the ring used to be. I had to take the ring off, you know, because of the arthritis, and now I can't get it back on again.

I told you that I'd stored the ring safely in that little shoebox where I keep all of my photographs and manuscripts from the old days; the days when I still had hope; the days when I had other people to compete against apart from you, apart from myself. The truth is; I don't know where the ring is. Maybe it's slipped through the bottom of the box and between the floorboards. Maybe it's in one of the pockets of my coat. I don't know. I swear I remember putting it on a different finger for a while, but my memory isn't what it used to be. Anyway, as I stared at my hand, I realised that this might have been what the medium was talking about. Maybe she'd spotted where my wedding band used to be, and guessed that I'd lost it. Maybe that would explain that secret power she'd held over me. Maybe that was her trick. Maybe she was simply a good observer.

Let me tell you about the allotments. I did not buy the small plot of land down by the river as I told you I had. The university bought it for me as a leaving present. Maybe they feared that I'd continue to hang around like a bad smell until they found me something else to do. I'd once told them that I was a keen gardener on some job application or other, and had had to keep up the pointless lie for over thirty years at the place. The keen gardener was actually my father. Now he had green fingers; no, maybe that's not right. Green fingers would imply that he had some of magic touch which was as much about luck as it was anything else. What he really had was commitment; he was thoroughly prepared to put in the back-breaking hours on his knees in the mud for the meagre return of a few cabbages or garden peas. But how sweet did they taste? Honestly – and I use the word advisedly – they tasted like nectar. When I was a child, I cracked open the pods and ate the hard, tiny peas as though they were sweets.

I've never had to worry about any of the local layabouts stealing into *my* allotment and pilfering the fruits of my own labour. The soil seems to be too rocky here. No matter how many times I rake through it and fill my wheelbarrow with what looks like the remnants of some archaeological dig, I still turn up more stones, trinkets and bottles the next time I'm down there. It is unforgiving work; maybe the land has taken a dislike to me. Nothing can be bothered to grow there. Sometimes, in spring, I'll see the first shoots of the spring onions, or the flowering of the peas, and I'll think *maybe this year*, but there's always something which causes them to wither and die. Sometimes it'll be an incredibly localised infestation of slugs, so I'll invest in bags and bags of the blue pellets. But it seems that they are special, nuclear-disaster-surviving slugs, and the poison has no visible effect on them. Sometimes, it'll be birds eating all of the foetal strawberries, and other times it'll be uncharacteristic torrential rain. That woman – the medium – had it right when she said that I sometimes call in at the supermarket and buy a few carrots or turnips and bring them home. I can't for the life of me understand why I feel the need to do this, but maybe it's got something to do with my whole problems with honesty. I don't want anyone, least of all you, thinking of me as a failure. If I could afford it, I'd have hired a gardener to take care of it for me. Can you imagine? What hobbies would I have then?

I hate the word 'hobby'; it makes what I'm doing seem downright petty. What I'm doing is in fact a penance, or so it seems. I hate the allotment, too, with its old down-to-earth *values* and hard work. What was supposed to be a space for relaxation has turned into some kind of open-air prison. When we go on holiday, I have to pretend that I've got old Bert to look in there for me; otherwise you'd start to smell a rat, wouldn't you? It feels like I've got an imaginary friend that I have to keep on making up more and more ludicrous stories about.

And so, I closed our front door and stepped down the road to the allotments. It's a fair walk, you know, and it takes me the best part of an hour to get there these days. I puffed and panted my way across town, sometimes holding onto the walls to get my breath back. All the time, I was thinking, *how much longer can I keep going with this lie?*

It was cold out, despite it being spring, and I could see my breath in front of my face as I opened the gate with a long, creaking sigh of resignation. As soon as I entered the allotment though, I could see that there was something different about the place. Underneath the knotted briar bush and by the clump of weeds in the corner – the corner where I hardly ever venture – was something green. I seemed to remember planting cabbages in that corner, a couple of years ago, but nothing ever showed, and it's become overgrown since then.

Moving as quickly as my old legs would carry me, I pressed forward into the allotment. There was a funny feeling in my stomach which I didn't recognise; I now know that the feeling wasn't my dinner repeating on me, but was in fact the first fluttering of something called hope. I knelt down in the soil and teased my fingers underneath the weeds, touching... a lettuce. It was a small, weak looking thing, but it was unmistakably a lettuce. And I'd grown it. Suddenly fearful that if I left it in the ground overnight, the slugs would get to it, I ripped it up out of the ground and stuck it into a plastic bag.

Walking home, I felt almost young. Excitement pumped through me and I swear that if anyone had seen me, they would have said that I had a spring in my step. You, of course, marched me straight back out of the kitchen and out of the back door when you saw that I'd tramped allotment mud across the hall carpet.

"How many times do I need to remind you to take your shoes off?" you said, not expecting a reply.

"Don't worry; I come bearing food," I grinned, tugging my old boot off and banging it against the wall to get rid of the mud which had clogged up the treads.

"A bit weedy-looking that lettuce isn't it?" you said, with a look of contempt on your face. But nothing would shake me out of my good mood. I even offered to wash it for you.

"Not likely," you said. "Just put the kettle on, if you don't mind."

I clicked on the kettle and leaned against the kitchen cabinet wearing a wide grin. I watched your back as it hunched over the sink. I watched you tear off the outer leaves of the lettuce, washing away the covering grey dust with the cold tap, massaging it into domesticity. Without looking up, you ripped into the heart of the lettuce, still vigorously washing the leaves. You were always so fastidious.

And then you stopped.

"Uuuurrrggghhh, there's something hard in here – it could be a snail shell or something."

You stopped washing the lettuce and indicated that I should take over. So, I rolled my sleeves up to my elbows and thrust my old hands into the sink. Who cares about the arthritis; I've grown this lettuce myself! My fingers touched that cold, hard thing that you'd found, hidden between the leaves. With a foolhardy smile, I pulled the thing out and saw it sparkle in the sunlight which streamed through the kitchen window. It was a ring. Quickly, I tried to shove the ring into my pocket before you could register that it was actually my lost wedding ring.

But you saw it too, didn't you? I found it quite difficult to read the expression that crossed your face. There was a flash of anger there, certainly; some thinly-veiled bitterness at my carelessness. There was something else there too, something that I'd not seen in you for years. I regret to say that I didn't have time to think what that expression really was. I was too busy worrying about what lie I was going to have to plant next; I knew that your questions would soon come thick and fast and that I had no idea how I was going to explain away the lost ring or why I'd not even told you it had been missing.

"I'm glad you've found what you were looking for," you said, quietly, not even looking at me.

And then I realised that you were crying; your shoulders were shaking. You were crying those awful, silent tears of somebody that has suffered greatly. You didn't expect comfort, weren't wailing your agony from the rooftops, you were simply crying. I wondered how many times you'd cried before and I hadn't noticed.

"I'm sorry," I breathed, the word feeling as unfamiliar in my mouth as the ring did in my hand.

You raised your eyes and looked at me. I took in the deep worry-lines in your forehead, the way your nostrils flare when you want to say something. I'd forgotten that, or never even looked recently. When you started to get those tell-tale creases by your mouth or crow's-feet by your eyes, I stopped looking. You became the unwanted reminder that time was chugging forward relentlessly, that dreams were futile. And I'm sorry that I made that connection; I'm sorry that I made you into an old woman.

"Why do we never talk any more? Why do you never tell me things?" you said.

"I... I... don't know," I replied.

You smiled an old-womanish smile and shook your head. And suddenly I knew, beyond all doubt what that look which had washed over you when you first saw the ring had been. It was hope, wasn't it? Some part of you wanted the ring to be a sign that we could still live 'happily ever after.' Maybe you hoped that there was something magical about the soil in the allotment this year; an added ingredient which would make everything grow just that little bit better.

I longed to kiss you then, to sweep you into my nurturing arms and make you grow again. But how do people ever get past the briars and brambles of the lies we tell? We start by sprinkling the small seeds of truth:

"I don't want to be old," I said. "I've been lying to myself for too long now. I just wanted you to know."

Ten years down the drain

The fifteenth of April flashed out like a neon sign in the middle of the calendar. It had been there at the back of my mind for so long that I'd started to get used to its Sword of Damocles-like intimidation. And so, almost without me noticing, it had crept up on me. Suddenly it was the twelfth, and I realised that I hardly had the time to even join a gym, let alone get in shape.

We'd agreed to meet at Juniper's, off Towler Street; you know the one? It's in all of the vegetarian eating guides; claims to be 'no frills' but is frequented by most of the rock bands that live in the area. So pretentious is Juniper's that it doesn't serve alcohol. Needless to say, Juniper's had been her choice of location. So much for the 'neutral ground' that she'd promised. She knew she'd be in her element while I'd be trying to drown out my nervousness by chewing the damn table-cloths.

I got there early and loitered by the bus stop. If she'd have seen me, I could have simply been pretending to be checking the timetable for a convenient bus home. As it was, I was hoping to catch a glimpse of her before she knew I was there; when she was 'au naturel', so to speak. Indeed, I'd somehow convinced myself that if I recognised her on the street and didn't have that old flutter of love and lust and anger and pain and hate in my belly that I might finally have gotten over her.

I was so early, in fact, that after a while, I had to take a seat inside the bus shelter, waving away at least three buses that I could have escaped on. While I waited, I stole stealthy looks at my cue-cards. I'd made sure that I'd written as much impressive material about my life now that she couldn't help but conclude how much better off I was without her. Although I did have to be careful not to make myself into some unattainable demi-god that she'd forever remember to be the 'one that got away'. I wanted her to decide that although she was not in my division, she was still in my league.

When a fourth bus pulled up at the stop, I decided that I'd better find a new place to do my loitering. It groaned to a halt so close to me that I could feel the dirty heat being produced by the engine. I motioned to the driver that I didn't want to board his bus no matter how many times he made the hydraulics hiss their frustration at me, but still he waited. Finally, the double-doors opened. I feared that I was about to be shouted at for wasting the driver's precious time and apologised profusely.

"Don't worry son," he said. "I wasn't waiting on you. Some bird on the top deck rang the bell, but she's playing silly beggars and won't get off now. I'll damn well wait until she does."

For a moment I stood by the bus and wondered whether further comment was required from me. The driver paid me no mind though, and carried on watching his little periscope thing which showed him the upper level of the bus. Eventually, he said: "Ah! Here comes the daft slapper now."

Dee emerged from the precariously steep steps of the double-decker trying manfully – womanmanfully – to appear composed while she tried to lug one of those unwieldy art portfolio cases and hold down her wildly flowery skirt and grip the railing all at the same time. My first impression of her was confused. On the one hand, I was delighted that it hadn't been me that was so flustered on the cusp of our meet, but on the other, I felt like I should leap onto the lip of the bus like some dashing knight and offer to assist the beautiful lady with her baggage.

Baggage; that was a pretty good description of my first impression of her; and I don't mean her belongings, I mean her general demeanour. Before she'd even spotted that I was standing outside the bus, I took in her severe new hairstyle, the tiredness in her eyes. Something about the way that she clutched onto the shabby remains of her bus-ticket convinced me that she wasn't rich, but had to scrimp and save her pennies, just like she always used to. Judging from her email, she should have arrived in a bloody limo, but here she was, relying on a DaySaverPlus like a single mother on benefits.

A sudden wave of nausea hit me then. I knew so little about her that she may well have been a single mother, struggling by on tuppence a week and the leftovers from whatever restaurant she worked in. My heart ached for her then, and I knew that I would step in at a moment's notice to be her little Tommy's father-figure. Maybe after a while I'd start to stay over, just so I could read him his bed-time story (he always liked it better when Uncle Danny read it; so much more passionate than mummy's tired drone). Maybe after a while longer, I'd start to sleep in Dee's bed again and I'd leave her to sleep in on a morning while I made all kinds of breakfast delights. We'd try for a sister for little Tommy after another year or so, and she'd be beautiful and talented and...

"Hello Daniel," said Dee, yanking me out of my reverie as though by the tuft of sticky-uppy hair at the front of my head.

Not for the first time in my life, or even that day - that minute - I was lost for words. Just how do you address over ten years of longing in a single coherent sentence?

As though to cover my embarrassment, the driver did the comradely thing and chose that moment to drive away, shaking his head as though in disbelief that "people like her can get out of bed of a morning, let alone get on a bus." I thought I caught a warning look in his eye.

Ignoring the prehistoric bellowing of the departing bus, Dee leaned over and planted a single whisper of a kiss on my cheek. I could already feel myself reddening. It's an appalling family trait that I'd be embarrassed to pass on to any children I have. At first, I feel this prickly heat all over, and then it becomes more localised. Cartoonishly, red blotches start to appear all over my cheeks. I know this because Dee once made me watch myself as my face clouded over in this way. I can't remember what she did to embarrass me, but I seem to recall the aftermath, when she tried to spot objects and faces in the blotches like children do with clouds.

"Clouding over again?" she said, grinning wildly.

And in that one moment, it felt as though the last ten years had never happened. I had to stop myself from reaching out and grabbing her around the waist.

"So? You going to help me with my baggage?" she asked.

I realised that I had still not spoken to her and was in danger of appearing like some common or garden idiot. I forced something out. A joke; surely you can't beat a good joke to smooth out the rough edges in an awkward situation. Get her laughing again. She always liked a good laugh.

"Have I got to be your psychiatrist again?" I asked dead-pan.

She looked at me coldly. I thought that I'd better have a go at explaining the joke or else I'd seem even more stupid.

"You know? Baggage? Psychiatrists?"

Dee shook her head at me. Suddenly I remembered that ten years *is* a long time. Who was I to know whether she had to go see a shrink these days? In fact, who was I to know about any of it? To be on the safe side, I decided right there and then to leave all of my usual stock-in-trade bitterly cynical remarks right there in the cynical old bus stop.

She handed me her art portfolio so that I couldn't see the contents. I waddled away from the bus stop in her wake, the case banging into my shins as I went. I caught her looking over her shoulder at me a couple of times, although it was exasperation written all over her features, rather than the hoped-for longing. We crossed the road and made for Juniper's like that; her leading the way, me bumbling behind like I was her embarrassing younger brother or something.

As we approached, I could see that most of the rock-star set were out in force. Despite the rather chilly spring weather, they were all sitting around small metal tables arranged in the middle of the pavement. When they stretched their legs, their ridiculous little winkle-pickers were dangling over the gutter. I saw a couple of old women having to virtually step into traffic in order to wheel their tartan shopping carts around these great sunglassioed oafs. I was so spitting with disgust at these boorish yobs that it took me a while to realise that Dee had indeed stopped to talk to one of them. I noted that she nodded over in my direction and one of this great swathe of leather-panted buffoons grimaced at her as though he shared her pain.

Almost unbeknownst to me, I realised that my old friend jealousy had come a-knocking, and as usual, I'd damn well gone and let him in again hadn't I? Instead of nonchalantly walking over and introducing myself, as I've done so many times since when I've replayed it in my head, I simply stayed by the menu sign and repetitively examined my watch. Finally, Dee remembered who she was supposed to be having lunch with and she bade goodbye to her choice of the stick-thin men. As she returned to me, I sucked in my paunch and tried to look cool.

"That wasn't very cool," she hissed at me. "Those guys have asked me to do some of the art-work for their new album cover. We could have joined them if you'd have not behaved like a jerk."

I grinned, meanly. "A jerk? What are you; American now?"

She knew exactly what I meant. I, of course, knew her from before her sudden adoption of that new accent mid-way through university. I knew that her real voice was more Bette Lynch than Bette Midler.

She sighed: "Let's go inside and find some dark little corner shall we? Like mould?"

I let that one go. I feared that if I pushed things any further she'd tell me to leave, and then I'd be left wondering what was going on with her and the tight-trousered philanthropist out there.

We found a table toward the back of the café which was rather too close to the cappuccino machine and its hissing echo of the bus's hydraulics for my liking, but I didn't want to labour the point. Here, there were still enough people surrounding us to prevent anything as backward as a full-on scene, which is clearly what she expected of me.

I propped the art portfolio against the leg of my chair and craned myself into the rather too small space which was left between me and the counter.

"Can't park yourself there love," said a waitress rushing by. "We need to get to the hatch."

"Where am I supposed to go then? In the toilets?" I muttered.

The waitress didn't hear me. Dee shot me a withering look. Awkwardly, I shuffled round the table a bit more. I was now virtually sitting on her knee, but she didn't seem to mind this as much as my making her look a fool with my cynical remarks. She always hated those cynical remarks.

She handed me a menu, probably so that I'd stop tearing at the paper table-cloth. "You'd have preferred it if we'd gone down to the pub, wouldn't you? But you can't even smoke in there these days, can you?"

Oh blessed opportunity! I hadn't needed all of the cue-cards in the end after all.

"Gave up smoking about eighteen months ago," I said, triumphantly and sat back and waited for the adoration to wash over me.

"Good for you," said Dee, picking up a menu of her own and starting to nosy on through the starters.

Hang on! Was this all she was going to say on the subject; the subject that had caused so many blazing rows between us? I remember her crying once when she woke up in the middle of the night and found me smoking in the darkness. She was worried that she'd have to live without me when I died of cancer. And now I'd done as she asked, all she could say was 'good for you.'

"It was a hard slog," I said, self-depreciatingly, "but in the end I came through and out the other end of that tunnel of crap. Like Andy Dufresne in *Shawshank*."

She always liked watching *Shawshank Redemption* with me. Or so I'd thought. Instead of smiling at the memory, she frowned.

"I hardly think that you can compare giving up smoking as being wrongfully imprisoned for something like twenty years and then making your..."

"Ah! That's where you're wrong. Smoking *was* like being in prison. It was..."

She interrupted back: "Let's just agree to disagree on this one. Think we can do that?"

Sometimes she behaved like she was my teacher, or parent. What was all that business with the 'we'? Think 'we' can do that? Again, I had to bite my tongue. While I tried to regain my calm I began revising my picture of Dee. Now I had the reason that she was a single mother; her new bloke was in prison. I stored away my conclusion for future reference.

Despite it being well past the traditional lunch-hour rush – Dee had always liked to keep a different routine to most of the rest of the world - the café was still a hive of activity. I'd once believed that there *was* a limit to how many smoothies or mochas or espressos that anyone could drink. Juniper's soon disabused me of that notion. People were treating the stuff as though it was holy water or something. While Dee stared at the menu, I tried not to listen to the snatches of conversation I heard from all around me. There were people talking about art exhibitions, theatre performances and the texture of the vegetarian food. I wondered if this was what they really wanted to talk about, or whether they simply felt that they had to in a place like this. I wondered if they would have much rather been talking about last night's football or why nobody ever watches *Eastenders* in *Eastenders*. I had some interesting views on that very subject, but didn't think that it would be the right time to share them with my lunch date.

"I think I'll have the stuffed peppers," said Dee, confidently closing the menu.

I chose to see the act as the challenge that it was most probably intended to be. I surfed my way down the menu; it was, I'm sure, being ironic or post-modern in the way that it placed photographs of each dish next to their descriptions. Nothing looked remotely appetising.

"I'm a big fan of stuffed peppers myself," I said. "I've even got to like aubergines, you know?"

Dee smiled. When she did so, her whole face seemed ten years younger. I could have been in a time machine if it weren't for her new haircut. Nevertheless, it was the first real sign of encouragement I'd had from her since my ill-advised jibe about psychiatrists. I decided that I had to build on that success.

"So; I've replaced the cigs with aubergines. What have you been doing in ten years?"

She gave a long drawn-out sigh as though weighing up how much to tell me. Finally: "Well, a lot of the time, I've been getting to know who I really am and what I want from life." She ran a hand through her short black hair and gave me this weary smile. I didn't jump in as I usually do, but allowed her the time to collect herself and continue.

"I know that you used to hate all of those people at university who went travelling to 'find themselves', but after you, I felt like I had to. I felt like I didn't know who I was any more. Do you know what I mean?"

I did know what she meant. I nodded, half-heartedly. I wanted to know more about what had happened to her *physically*, rather than spiritually or mentally.

"I've been living down here for most of the time since university, but I did spend some time living on a farm up in the Lake District," she continued, gesturing to the art portfolio, "and that's where I started painting."

And I was prepared to stake my meagre savings on the fact that she started a hell of a lot more up in the Lake District too. She always liked outdoorsy-types; I could imagine her taking up with some poet up there or something. For some reason, I discovered in that moment that I absolutely hated poets. And the Lake District. Luckily, the over-worked waitress chose that moment to attend to our table and I was distracted from my baser instincts by my sheer confusion at the sheer number of coffees which I was supposed to choose from.

"Just white; three sugars," I decided finally.

The waitress shoved herself past me and through the hatch, probably on her way to spitting in my drink. Dee looked at me in silence. Evidently I was supposed to enquire further as to her new talent.

"So is painting your line of work?" I asked.

"I wouldn't exactly call it work,' she said. 'I don't work. Not in the conventional sense anyway. I don't believe in all this capitalist accumulation nonsense. I'm not one for slaving my whole life just to pay for a roof over my head. I'm actually squatting in a friend's caravan at the moment."

"What friend?" I spurted out, rather too quickly.

"A *girl*friend," said Dee, raising her eyes to the ceiling in mock frustration. "Honestly, Daniel, anyone would think that we're still together."

For a long moment, we sat in silence.

"So what is it you do?" she asked, finally.

I remembered the cue-card. "I'm actually doing okay for myself. Got a nice little copy-writing business going. I *slave* away at it so I can pay for the pile of bricks I got myself out in the 'burbs. I'm pretty much Mr. Capitalist Nonsense himself."

This time it was Dee's turn to respond rather too quickly: "I didn't mean anything by that remark. It's just that I'm not cut out for traditional lines of work."

"More of a free spirit?" I grinned. Because that had always been how I'd seen our relationship. She was flighty; other-worldly and I was the one that grounded her. Perhaps she saw it as me dragging her down to my level, but 'solid grounding' was how I saw it; I stopped her from just floating away into the either. Which was, it seemed, exactly what had happened to her.

"I'm not just some innocent," she said.

"I know; I miss you for you," I admitted, before I'd realised that the thought had even passed my lips.

Amazingly, she reached across the table and took my hand. Her hand wasn't as I'd remembered it. It was coarser now; more lived in. There were still traces of paint on her long fingers.

"You're not still holding out a hope for us, are you?" she asked slowly. "Because we're both different people now."

I let her voice soothe me. In a trance-like state, I hardly listened to her imparting the bad news once again.

"Because our relationship was a tired old love story which limped on way past the time when only amputation was the only thing that would cure us," she continued. "Instead of discovering the world, we rotted together in the flat. We watched our dreams grow so gangrenous that even our friends sensed the aroma of decay in the air around us and so let us alone."

I remembered the basement flat. I remembered the glory days of doing nothing because we had each other. We basked in bed all day long, like sea-lions. We locked the door on the outside world, only occasionally drawing the curtains and blinking confusedly at the raging August heat. When we pulled our sticky bodies away from each other in September, we agreed that we had to part. No recriminations. We simply went our separate ways and entered the world like new-borns.

"I had to end it, Danny, or we'd have ended up ruining each other for ever," she said.

"But that was just a trial. We had to find jobs and do things and then we'd get back together. I thought we both wanted that long summer after Uni again. There's a lovely garden at my new place…"

"Your memory is playing tricks on you. What do you really remember of that long summer? Sure *you* stayed in our pit all day long, but I crept away and sat on the front stairs like the poor abandoned flower that cranes its neck to a room's only sliver of sunlight, hoping for some nourishment."

I snorted my disbelief. *She* was the one whose memory was playing tricks. I pulled my hand away, suddenly disgusted with myself for showing my weakness. For as soon as I'd shown it, she had leaped right back in to her old ways; that rather unbecoming habit she had of making me feel guilty for holding her back, as though I'd been some kind of tyrant. I wouldn't have stopped her from going outside if she'd wanted to.

She thought she'd won again, didn't she? She thought she could manipulate my feelings once more.

"What's the matter now?" she asked. "You look as though you are trapped by love and hate."

I sighed. Maybe Dee wasn't such a new person after all. She had retained just about every annoying habit that she'd had when we were together, including colouring everything she said with this pretentious jargon which seemed to come straight from *Bitch* magazine's summer self-help book or whatever other clap-trap she happened to be reading.

I tried to be reasonable.

"I shouldn't have said that about missing you," I said. "Just forget I even said it."

"It was a sweet thing to say, as long as it was for the right reasons," she said softly. Before I could even respond, the waitress called out that our order was ready to collect from the counter.

"Why can't she give us table service like everyone else?" I hissed.

"That's just for the customers outside," said Dee. "Look; would you mind getting these, only I've already told you I don't have a job."

She fluttered her eyelashes and I meekly obeyed. I sloped over to the counter and handed over the exorbitant fee for the sad-looking portions on our plates. While I was waiting for my change – and I'm sure the waitress took twice as long as she needed to in order that I'd say 'keep it' – I looked back at Dee at our table. She was staring resolutely at a message on her mobile phone; a dark frown had crossed over her forehead. Bad news?

The waitress handed me my change on a saucer, perhaps hoping that this would embarrass me into leaving her a tip, but I picked it up and poured the contents into the palm of my hand. She tutted quite audibly as I picked up the tray and returned to my table. My next coffee, if there was to be one, would be laced with rat poison rather than spittle.

I manoeuvred the tray onto the small table and tried to find somewhere to put the menu and condiments which was not the centre of my plate.

"I'm going to have to make a move straight after we eat," said Dee. "I've had an urgent message and I need to, you know, do something about it."

I pretended to concentrate on the task of sawing into the tough red pepper, hoping that she would elaborate, but she said nothing more on the matter.

"You got me here under false pretences," I said, though a mouthful of cheese. "All you want me for is my money."

Perhaps I hoped she would laugh. Perhaps I hoped she would tell me the real reason she wanted to see me. Whatever I hoped, it certainly wasn't that she start crying. She cried the silent tears of a person that has cried too much for one lifetime. She dropped her fork right into the middle of the stuffed pepper and blew out her cheeks.

"Don't you understand? I don't want anything from you. I don't want your money or your emails. I don't want your concern. I don't want…"

"You emailed me," I snapped. I was right on this point. In a court of law, if they had to ascertain which one of us was responsible for us being in this miserable lunch date, they would conclude that she had made the first move. Sure there were all of the other emails I'd sent, but this lunch had been her idea.

"Why can't you remember all of the misery when we ended?" she asked, through a fog of tears. I glanced around nervously to check whether anyone else in the café had noticed. They hadn't; still lost in their discussions of Stanislavski and his system. "Don't you recall your drunken phone calls?" she continued. "All of the times I had to stay on the line for hours for fear that you would commit your threatened suicide if I hung up?"

Commit my threatened suicide? The dismissive way that she'd spat that out of her mouth pretty much summed up where she believed the balance of power lay now. She didn't think that I meant anything that I'd said. Ever. The realisation hit me between the eyes like a train. Fast, I re-discovered the fact that my hope was unfounded.

"I'm sorry," I moaned. "I won't pester you like that again."

"I don't mean *that*," she said, still exasperated, still crying. "I just wanted to know that you were happily on with your life and that you've forgotten about me. But you're still there, aren't you? You are still the man you were ten years ago?"

Finally my own tears came. I couldn't stop them. Everything she said was true. I stumbled away from the table, knocking over her art portfolio in my haste to get away, and made for the toilet. I couldn't let the damn waitress see me like that.

As I pushed my way into the toilet, I stole one last look over my shoulder and saw the slumped shoulders of Dee leaving Juniper's. It was such a familiar sight; the amount of times I'd reduced her to such defeat was despicable. I was despicable.

When the toilet door swung shut behind me, I realised that I was not alone in there. But male-bathroom etiquette dictates that you can't very well back out of such a place; not of there is a spare urinal; not if you don't want people wondering why you've backed-out and what you might have to hide; and certainly not when the other inhabitant of the room is one of the stick-thin, leather-trousered, winkle-pickered sunglassioed buffoons from one of the tables outside. Indeed, the more I stared at him, the more I decided that he was the very one that Dee had been speaking with when we had first arrived.

I ambled up to the urinal, staring at the tiles, trying with everything I had not to make eye-contact. He'd surely see that I'd been crying.

Too late.

"You were with Dee. How d'ja know her?" he said. He was leaning backwards as he urinated, legs wide apart. He oozed confidence.

I didn't say anything.

He asked again. I could see that he'd finished urinating now, but he still stood next to me, not zipping-up.

"You know Dee?" he repeated.

I answered finally, sensing that he wouldn't leave me alone until I at least acknowledged his presence. "We go way back." I felt like adding 'unlike you' in brackets.

"Whassyer name then squire?"

For a moment I felt like lying, but really, what was the point?

"Danny," I muttered.

"Really; Danny? Danny Morris?"

"Yeah," I replied, warily.

"Oh, I've heard so much about you man,' he said. 'Dee's always telling us funny stories about you."

I dreaded to think.

"She told us all about your witty remarks and all that, although she swore she could never do them justice when she said them. She told me all about how you got together and all of the stuff you used to talk about. You inspired her, man."

I was speechless. I met his eyes, tried to ascertain whether he was being sarcastic or not. He wasn't. I could tell straight away.

"I miss her," I said, sadly.

"Aw, some people just ain't meant to be together, man. It don't mean you're a bad person."

He left me in the toilet, still gripping the towel. When I caught a glimpse of myself in the mirror, I had those awful red blotches all over my face again, only now it was tears again.

I still had a chance.

A.J Kirby

By Hook or by Crook

By hook or by crook, I'll be first in this book, Dad scrawled in that doctor's handwriting of his that I'd come to know, but not necessarily love. He crammed the writing into the top left hand corner of the inside front cover, above the printer's details. I hated it; even then, I knew it was a trite, condescending little rhyme which was unbecoming of a man in his position.

He wrote it as a joke, of course. He chuckled in that gruff, moustache-sucking way of his as he did it; he had a look about him which plainly said that he'd been planning it all along. And then he scribbled his signature underneath, and that was worse; just a vague rendering of his initials, swallowed up by some unnecessary loop-de-looping of the pen. I hated it so much that I would not even allow it to be called an autograph; it was a signature.

"You're not famous enough to have an autograph," I sneered, as I flounced out of the front room, leaving him still clutching the book, still drowning in the wrapping paper which had been discarded from my mountain of presents. I watched through the crack in the door as he sighed and took another swallow of beer. He was probably drunk, I thought, and that was why he was being so uncharacteristically foolish – boisterous even.

Amongst the murderous robots, the fighting dinosaurs, the bike and the football kit, you would have expected something as old-fashioned as an autograph book to have been completely ignored. But there was something about that book; for one, it looked like the big red book from *This is Your Life*, but it was more than that. Compared to the reverse side of the thin, pock-mark edged computer paper on which I usually stored my ideas, the book was like a glorious, rich new world. It must have been like discovering papyrus after years of graffitiing on walls. It was an elaborately bound book, with heavy pages which I later found to be called bond paper. All of those clean, white, virgin pages! With no bold type shining through from the other side! It was like paper heaven.

Excited by my initial response to the book, Dad had started to tell me that it was just like the book which he would loyally bring to the Test Matches of his youth at fabled places like Old Trafford and Headingley.

"Ah, I wished I'd kept that book in a safe place," he said, with a faraway look in his eyes. "All of those names, all of those memories. It'd be like smelling the warm beer and the cut grass of my youth…"

I didn't really know what he was talking about then, and blamed it on the beer, but I know now. I know how much it meant to him now.

"Would you let me sign it?" he asked, hopefully. "My dad signed mine when he gave it to me…"

And then he went and spoiled it all with his stupid little rhyme.

At first, I stubbornly refused to even look at the book again, but something about that lavish red cover drew me back in after a while. And I swear that Dad kept laying it around so that I'd almost trip over it in the bathroom, or mistake it for a box of chocolates in the cupboard. There was something about that book. Finally, I forgave him for his terrible mistake and I started to collect signatures. And oh could I collect! Like the football stickers and the *Star Wars* figures, the signatures became something that I just had to have more of. I would traipse around neighbours, teachers, even the dentist - in fact, all of the adults I knew in my young life - and I'd collect their writings. Of course, I wouldn't allow any of my friends sign it – not after the mess they'd made of my plaster-cast after I'd broken my arm.

Eventually, the pages show me that I moved on from the Minor League and I was soon batting above my weight in the Majors. Baseball was my sport, not cricket; we were in America now after all. My book was filled with the scrawls of the almost impossibly famous New York Yankees players… And of course the Kit Men, the Assistant Managers, the journalists who were also waiting for the players to emerge from the changing rooms and enter that rugby scrum of a car park at the old training ground. I wasn't discerning any more; I'd take anyone… as long as they were connected with Baseball.

Each day, as training ended, I'd be just one amongst a baying mob of children, all looking to fill their own books. The place had a heavy smell of deep-heat ligament oil and I'm sure it made us all light-headed. Half of us didn't even recognise the players we were that excited, and hence we'd just take anyone's signature. Oh, the players found it a drag alright. You could see that tightness around their jaws which showed their annoyance. But they bore it with good grace; it was par for the course. It was only midday after all, and the rest of the day was theirs to drink away, to plant firmly in the bottom left hand pocket of the pool table, or to simply sleep.

Now I work fifteen hour shifts down at the law firm and I have seen enough bond paper to last me two lifetimes. I would swap my right arm to be in a position to just stand around, shooting the breeze, signing some kid's autograph book. To me, signatures are now pledges, guarantees, warranties, proof. They are ties, authentication; people sign their lives away when they scrawl on my papers. I watch them as they chew the end of the pen, blow out their cheeks and try not to cry as they identify themselves as the people who have lost everything.

These days nobody has autograph books any more. The kids outside the brand spanking new suburban training complex – more like a military facility - of the Yankees have to wait by the side of the road, outside the reinforced perimeter gates. They bring with them the Baseball caps, shirts, photographs and programmes which they then put up for sale on e-bay. The personal message is now frowned upon by the discerning autograph hunter. It has become a professional get-rich quick scheme, rather than an amateur, fun pursuit; you get more money for the blank, universal message than the personal.

Can you imagine if you were trying to sell a shirt with the legend – 'Hey Dickie, Keep up the arm-work, Cheers, blah, blah, blah' emblazoned across it? How many Dickies' do you know? Exactly. And so, the kids find that it's worth risking having your arm chopped off by a rhinoceros-sized Hummer if you can get the star-pitcher's signature on a ball – it can fetch hundreds of dollars on the open market, but they also beg and plead that it's a secret present and they don't want the name on it… or they call it luck… anything. You'd be lucky if you found a Dickie in America that would also be interested in buying your ball.

Dad called me Dickie after the cricket umpire Dickie Bird. Even then, it was rather an old-fashioned name, and I begged to be known as Richard. But Dad told me that I'd grow into the name; Dickie Twist; it made me sound as though I was one of Oliver's younger brothers in the Dickens Novel – I was a nineteenth century nearly-man, not a twentieth century star, which is what I so wanted to be. I used to practice my signature. Elaborate loops and curls, loping t's and daringly dashing d's. Unfortunately, I could never reproduce any of the signatures, and neither could I do them quickly. It wasn't a star's signature. Star's signatures were unthinking crosses, absent-minded dashes across the page and onto the next one… I wasn't a star.

I used to get teased about my name, but father told me that it was just jealousy. It was because I had a name that was destined to be famous, he'd say. He said that he could see the name up in lights – for what, I never really knew. I suppose that's why he bought me the autograph book, though, to make me see that I could belong in such exalted company. Maybe he wanted to help me on the way.

I suppose I am a star now, in terms of the law, in terms of sheer client hours I accrue every damn year. But I don't think you'll ever see a lawyers name up in lights, do you? When Dad died, it literally knocked all of the stuffing out of me. Suddenly, that great Rock of Gibraltar that had loomed over my every move wasn't there any more. I remembered, too late, that I also loved the man.

I loved him for the stupid phrases he'd repeat as he knocked about the house on a Saturday morning before baseball practice. I loved him for the way that he cried like a baby at movies which I thought were pretty stupid. I loved him for how he'd looked after me when Mom went back to England. And I loved him for the promise of a better life for me; a promise that was always on his lips.

Hell, I didn't even have any photographs of him in the apartment, so I had to go to the Storage Depot to have a look at some of my old things to try and find him. Why had I completely wiped him out of my life? I'd always thought that it was because of him; because of the way that he was; later, he'd drunk more and more. Now I realise that he missed Mom, that was all, and our Cold War was entirely my fault.

I dug out the old autograph book and blew off the dust. For some reason, I opened the book the wrong way up, but maybe it was Dad's hand, prompting me again, for do you know what I found?

By hook or by crook, I'll be last in this book.

He'd crammed the message right into the corner of the very bottom of the page, in tiny writing. It would be impossible to crow-bar another message in underneath. Dad was right – he was last in the book. It was the most important message.

A.J Kirby

Distance

Let me measure the distance between us. Let me evaluate this vastness of space and time like an oceanographer. Let me map out the wax and wane of our separation. You know that I work with figures, solid truths, but what equation could describe how we have drifted apart? What compass could express my yearning to be close to you again?

I could count the revolutions of the trundle wheel, but there would be so many clicks it would be like trying to calculate the number of random finger-snaps by a whole football stadium of Fonzies. I could fire off a depth charge, deep under the surface of us; see a three-dimensional rendering of the yawning chasm which slices through our hearts, but I couldn't bridge that gap. Now, even when I am with you, we are not together.

You hate these uncomfortable weekends. You must have come to think of them as prison-time in recompense for a crime which you did not commit. Like the Count of Monte Cristo you imagine a daring escape, but can't quite bear to punish you gaoler so. Remember how I used to read you that text? Remember how excitement curled around you like a cat's tail?

How can I impress you now? How can I travel that well-worn path into your good books once more; do I need to beg? Maybe I should. Maybe you'd be satisfied with my grovelling. It would give you that sense that everything was right and natural in the world again.

And so, when I come to you, I'm Sting's Englishman in New York. I'm alone and alien and, dare I say it, a little apathetic in my arthritic attempts at a connection. Perhaps I too have given up. You're a hard-faced urban sophisticate that I can't hope to compete with these days. You're always name-dropping, dwarfing my petty little efforts to interest you. You're a collator of foot-notes; always ready to reference some of the real celestial bodies that populate your life nowadays. I hardly even recognise you.

It goes on and on. You'll say: "Oh, I saw blah, blah in the deli. We did lunch." And I'll scratch at my beard and rack my brains as to where I might have heard that name before; which in-flight magazine might have featured that particular star? As I'm doing this, you'll perform that exaggerated rolling of your eyes that was once the bane of my life. It pains me to see you looking so tired, so worldly. You were never worldly; I always used to feel that if I wasn't holding you so tightly, you'd float off into the air, never to be seen again.

"You don't know who I'm talking about, do you?" you'll sigh. Your disgruntled breath will be thick and foggy in the cold air.

Inside, I'll be screaming. I don't *do* lunch like you do. It's too much of a leap for me. The only things I *do* are these eternal flights; this crazy-ass acquisition of air-miles and bags under my eyes. I do not do things like lunch. Lunch is something that just happens, like breathing.

So, we'll sit in silence for a while, and you'll think about art and I'll think about science. Maybe I'll lightly touch your knee or reach out for your gloved hand. We're both aware that time is trudging relentlessly onwards and it is our duty to make of that time what we will. And we do try, don't we? We try to keep up appearances in the best English tradition. I hand you your lean sandwich and tuck in to my own now-cold grease-burger. We huddle into the bench and try to find things that we can talk about. We remark that all things are "nice", that the air here at Harlem Meer is somehow cleaner than in the rest of New York.

You look as though you have been crying out for some good old-fashioned fresh air. It puts the colour back in your cheeks; makes you look more natural somehow and not so grey and urban. It softens the features of your face and brings that dancing light back to your eyes.

"I'm going away in the summer," you say, suddenly. Your voice is pitched somewhere in the mid-Atlantic now, and seems coldly unfamiliar. "California State let me in despite what happened in the fall."

"It'll be on account of your connection to the famous Dr. Grey," I joke, trying to play down my agony at the thought of even more distance being placed between us.

You don't laugh though; you're all-business. "I'm not doing physics, Roger," you say. I hate it when you call me Roger; it seems so impersonal. I hate it almost as much as the fact that you've now adopted the American spelling of your name, replacing the 'e' with an 'a'.

"Don't go," I whisper.

"I have to go," you say. "I'm meeting someone."

You're bored of me. I know that. It's a matter of scale, I think. I can't get my head around America or the new you that inhabits it. It feels as large as the solar system to me. Why can't you understand how distances make me feel?

"I'll walk with you," I say.

You just nod your head. But you don't move. It is as though there is something more that you want to say. I know that feeling only too well, and so I sit in silence and let you compose yourself. In the silence, I become aware of a lonely bird singing its sad lament in a nearby cypress tree. Maybe he's trying to tell me something about loss. Maybe he's asking: "how far is too far?"

"See that bird in the tree?" I ask. I've given you ample opportunity to speak, but you just can't find the words, can you? Well, let me do it for you. "Imagine that bird has a tiny flea riding in the feathers. If this bench is the sun, that flea is Mercury."

"What are you talking about, Roger?" you ask, getting that look on your face.

I creak up from the bench and start to measure out thirty long steps away from you. Then, and with some triumph in my voice, I spin round and face you again, shouting: "Venus!"

Wearily, you climb to your feet too. You trudge after me as though wearing a ball and chain attached to your feet. But when you reach me, I notice the traces of a small smile playing on your lips. You remember this, don't you? Our little games?

"Earth?" you ask.

I begin this crazy long stride as though I'm in Monty Python. Unbelievably, you start to follow; bouncing along as though you're walking on the moon. You look so foolish! It's so long since I've seen you not care about what anyone would think of you...

We move out of the park; Earth is on 108th Street and Mars is only a few more giggly moon-steps from there. We walk so close that our steps fall into sync; we're both caught up in this current of desire for things not to be as they are. We are both mapping out our reconnection. But maybe I'm mistaken; maybe I'm reading too much into things. For there is a bit of distance between Mars and Jupiter, and your pace soon begins to slacken. By the time we reach Madison Avenue - the rough approximation of where you used to get bored when we used to play

Planets – you've stopped the giggles and got that bored look in your eyes. Back then, you used to ask me whether we were nearly there yet; ridiculously, I'd always make you ask the question in a different way, not like all the other kids ask.

By 110th Street, even I've given up walking like an astronaut. It's become all about the destination rather than the journey once more. But then you do something that is completely unexpected; you surprise me. Did you actually comprehend how happy it would make me when you stoop to pick up that dime from the floor or was it pure accident?

"This is Jupiter," you say, holding up the dirty coin for me to see. I beam with pleasure; how perceptive of you! If Mercury is only a flea on a bird's back, then you are right to scale up for Jupiter. Maybe we'll make a Scientist out of you yet… although I'm not sure if that's what you have in mind.

Along East 110th, much further down, we also find Saturn. I finger a button on your expensive duffel coat to show the planet's scale, but somehow you don't seem that enamoured with the game any more. We don't talk much as we plot a course into the nether reaches of our solar system; turning right at Frederick Douglass Circle and then right again into West 110th Street. The discovery of Uranus should have cheered you up. "Your anus!" you used to screech, loving the excuse to use a dirty word with impunity. Now though, you are dangerously quiet.

Neptune is on Morningside Drive and Pluto way out on Amsterdam Avenue.

"Pluto's not even classed as a planet any more," I say, trying to inject a little more interest into things again. But you don't even respond. Please understand, love, how small I really am. I am the tiny little Pluto, orbiting your sun. You can't even see me. I'm ice-cold from lack of your warmth. Hell, they've even changed my classification now, like you changing the spelling of our name.

"And now, Lisa, do you know where we might find the closest star to the sun?" I ask, before answering my own question as is my wont. "Well, if we were keeping to the same scale as we have just walked the solar system, it would be as far away as Los Angeles. Now do you see why I don't want you to go?"

"Don't talk to me like I'm still a child, dad," you say. "Los Angeles isn't Proxima Centauri. That was just a silly little game we played years and years ago before you decided that your work was more important than your family."

"But don't you see? It's all about space," I shout, but already you are orbiting some new sun. A boy I'd hardly noticed before steps out of one of the proliferation of theatres and links your arm. He's tall and broad shouldered and not at all grey. He holds you as I once did, so there's no distance at all between you. You've only got eyes for each other, you and him, your Los Angeles boy.

And you never even thought to introduce me. As you float away through space and time I feel something break within me. My heartstrings have been stretched and stretched but now they have snapped. *That* is the distance between us, I think.

A.J Kirby

Also by A.J Kirby

BULLY
Published by Wild Wolf Publishing, 2009

They say you should never go back. But sometimes you don't have a choice.

After Gary Bull's miraculous survival from an explosion out in Afghanistan, he is forced to return to the small town where he grew up. Forced to confront a past that he thought he had buried forever. Forced to face the horror of what he did when he was young. The bullying.

Welcome to Newton Mills, a town with more than its fair share of graveyards; a town where the skeletons are liable to walk right on out of the closet.

The scene of the crime.

Bully is the vivid, deeply disturbing story of being buried alive in Nowheresville, UK, and the psychological scars which have been left on the people there.

In a place where death surrounds everything, can anyone really be free?

Buy now from: www.andykirbythewriter.20m.com

THE MAGPIE TRAP
Published by Youwriteon.com/ Legend Press, 2009

Danny Morris wakes up on the sofa with the furred-tongue and pounding headache of a serious hangover. On the coffee table is the sorry evidence of the previous night's festivities; the mostly empty bottle of whisky, the overflowing ashtray and the greasy pizza box. There's something else there too; the bag of money, loot from one of the most audacious heists undertaken in modern times.

A.J Kirby's *The Magpie Trap* is a high-octane crime thriller in which a band of unlikely criminals discover a technical loop-hole which will allow them to walk out of Edison's Printers, carrying with them the famous Precisioner printer – the world's most powerful bank-note printer.

Undertaking one of the most audacious heists in modern times is not usually something that people scribble in to their dog-eared lists of 'things to do before you're thirty'. Nevertheless, as real life and responsibility close in on our three unhappy heroes, that is exactly what they find themselves planning to do.

Will they get away with their crime? Will the money bring them a better life? Or will the dogged ex-detective Jim Hunter pick up their scent? Can they escape the magpie trap?

Buy now from: www.andykirbythewriter.20m.com

Mix Tape

A.J Kirby

Mix Tape

www.ingramcontent.com/pod-product-compliance
Lightning Source LLC
Chambersburg PA
CBHW020337260626
47156CB00004B/1563